Shay took two steps outside the door then felt Quinn grab her hand and hold tight. She stopped.

It was obvious she wasn't going anywhere. He turned her around and pulled her flush against the solidness of his body. She gasped, immediately feeling his hardness pressed up against her as he sandwiched her between his body and the door frame. She looked up into his dark stormy eyes as he leaned close. Then, just inches away, he paused and whispered two words. "Please stay."

She opened her mouth to speak, but in one smooth swift motion, he cupped and angled her head to meet his. The kiss was instant and his tongue delved deeply into her mouth as soon as their lips touched. She surrendered, wrapping her arms around his neck and holding tight. She felt a surge of passion erupt throughout her body. It had been too long, and right now she never wanted this feeling to end. As the kiss deepened, she pressed closer and pulled harder, molding her body to his as much as she possibly could. Being closer to him was all she could fathom.

Books by Celeste O. Norfleet

Kimani Romance

Sultry Storm
When It Feels So Right
Cross My Heart
Flirting with Destiny
Come Away with Me

Kimani Arabesque

Love is for Keeps
Love After All
Following Love
When Love Calls
Love Me Now
Heart's Choice

Kimani TRU

Pushing Pause
She Said, She Said
Fast Forward

CELESTE O. NORFLEET

a native Philadelphian, has always been artistic, but now her artistic imagination flows through the computer keys instead of a paintbrush. She is a prolific writer for Kimani Arabesque and Kimani Romance. Her romance novels, realistic with a touch of humor, depict strong sexy characters with unpredictable plots and exciting story lines. With an impressive backlist, she continues to win rave reviews and critical praise for her sexy romances that scintillate, as well as entertain. Celeste also lends her talent to the Kimani TRU young-adult line. Her young-adult novels are dramatic fiction, reflecting current issues facing African-American teens. Celeste lives in Virginia with her husband and two teens. You can contact her at conorfleet@aol.com or P.O. Box 7346, Woodbridge, VA 22195-7346 or visit her website at www.celesteonorfleet.com.

Come AWAY with Me

CELESTE O. NORFLEET

To Fate & Fortune

KIMANI PRESS™

Recycling programs for this product may not exist in your area.

ISBN-13: 978-0-373-86202-3

COME AWAY WITH ME

www.kimanipress.com

Printed in U.S.A.

Dear Reader,

Who wouldn't love to experience a new adventure? I know I would, so I wanted to make sure that in writing *Come Away with Me* that's exactly what you'd get. The story introduces you to Shay Daniels and Dr. Quinn Anderson. After years of disappointing relationships, Shay is just plain tired. She needs rejuvenating, reinvigorating and, most of all, romance. Quinn is a therapist on a mission to help others, since he can't seem to help himself. They meet at a point in their lives when they least expect to find love but are in desperate need of it. Both have their own agendas, but when love intersects there's no point in fighting it.

I hope you enjoy their romance, along with a scenic tour of Tucson, Arizona, and the Serenity Resort & Spa. It's an oasis of beauty for broken and troubled hearts. Allow yourself to get swept away as love opens their hearts and, hopefully, yours.

Blessings & Peace,

Celeste O. Norfleet

Chapter 1

As her car turned off the main highway, Shay Daniels looked out of the window, searching for some kind of landmark. She continued driving, hoping to reach her final destination shortly. In the distance up ahead she could see the resort where she would be spending the next two and a half weeks. She still couldn't believe she was finally on vacation. It was a long-awaited, long-expected and definitely long-overdue break. Now she was finally here.

Serenity Resort and Spa was certainly breathtaking. But to her, it was nothing special. She was used to luxurious resorts set in spectacular locales. She gave a half smile as she removed her dark sunglasses to get a better view. Like so many other places, she was sure it was all hype and little substance. She'd been there, done that, and she'd seen it all before.

Serenity Resort was perched high atop a hill, nestled against the background of Arizona's Tucson Mountains and surrounded by the Sonora Desert and mountain range. But like all the other resorts she'd been to before, it was just another place where the reality never quite measured up to the expectation. It offered nothing new. She paused. She hadn't even given the place a chance. Perhaps she really was becoming too cynical.

As the host of the Romance Channel's most popular show, *Romantic Destinations,* she was used to stunning venues. Finding and covering the best honeymoon havens and idyllic locations for romance was her job. And she did it extremely well. Once an episode of her show aired, the featured resort was nearly always guaranteed a boost in guests. She could practically pick and choose the places she wanted to review. She'd wanted to feature Serenity Resort before, but the owners hadn't accepted her offer.

Over the course of three years, Shay had traveled to just about every exotic destination around the world and interviewed hundreds of couples about their weddings, honeymoon plans and romantic getaways. But not this time, because this trip was different. This wasn't business; it was personal, something just for her and she needed it.

The show was on hiatus and she was exhausted. It was her first real, *almost* do-nothing vacation in years. The *almost* part had to do with an article she'd promised to write for the Romance Channel's website run by her friend Jade Copeland, the site's editor-in-chief.

It had been the vacation she'd planned to take with her boyfriend—now *ex-boyfriend.* That was nearly a year ago, and it had taken that long to clear both their busy schedules and make the reservation. It was going to be their time together to renew their relationship. But apparently he couldn't wait that long. He'd dumped her six months ago and moved on. The vacation was already paid for in full, so she'd decided to go anyway.

Actually, there was more to it than that. She needed the time to reassess what had gone wrong. Running away really wasn't her style, but she knew she had to do something. She needed to get out of New York City and relax, refocus. With eight million people, the city still wasn't big enough. And Shay found out the hard way at dinner with Jade just before her vacation.

Midway through a perfect chocolate mousse, she noticed her ex-boyfriend Bruce walk into the restaurant with what looked like an inflatable Barbie doll. It was the first time she'd seen him in months. He calmly walked over to their table, introduced his fiancée and then gave Shay the "We're all adults here, so can't we still be friends?" speech. "Sure," she'd told him. "Why not?" But she knew that wasn't going to happen.

"Can you believe he actually told me I was cynical and emotionally detached?" she said indignantly, as she'd watched Bruce and his fiancée walk away from their table. It was pure psychobabble as far as she was concerned. It was clear that he was looking for a way out and the self-help books and seminars gave him exactly the justification he needed.

"He actually told you that," Jade said.

Shay nodded. "Yeah, how crazy does that sound? Me, of all people. Do you believe it? All those stupid self-help books have really gone to his head. He really thinks he's some kind of shrink. Why didn't he just admit to himself that he cheated on me, plain and simple?"

"Come on, Shay, this is me. The truth is you have become a bit jaded lately," Jade said. Shay opened her mouth to protest.

"Oh, come on, don't act so offended. You know it's true. And before you say anything, I'm telling you this as your best friend. You have lost your sense of optimism. You used to love your job at the network and it showed. I don't see that anymore. It's like you've forgotten what romance is all about.

"Look, I'm not saying it's crazy wrong, I understand it. You know I understand it. Every guy you've ever dated has dumped you and lately you've been damn near carrying the whole show. You do the research, you edit, you host and in your spare time you write pieces for the website. That's a lot for one person. Granted, the show is the better for it and so is the website, but in doing all that, where does that leave you?"

"Alone again," she said solemnly.

"Exactly. Now where does it say that's right? It used to be that when you interviewed couples on the show you were full of excitement. You interviewed with your heart and it showed. Now you just seem to go through the motions without ever feeling what you're reviewing. It's called the Romance Channel for a reason, remember. It's like you don't even believe in love anymore, let alone the possibility of a lasting relationship. But that's exactly what we're supposed to be selling."

"You mean the whole happily ever after scenario?" she deadpanned.

Jade nodded.

Shay shrugged. "I don't know, maybe I don't believe anymore. I guess getting dumped three times in a row can do that to you. I go on assignment and see all these couples who believe they've found the perfect love, and just because they go to some romantic resort they think it'll last forever. They're wrong. Do you know how many emails I get from those same people telling me they've separated or divorced? Too many," she said. "It makes me wonder why I even bother."

"Good Lord, it's even worse than I thought," Jade said. "Shay, the show is predicated on love and romantic getaways. How can you possibly be excited about a romantic location when there's not a romantic bone in your body anymore? You're the writer and the host. Our audience is supposed to see the joy of romance reflected in you. They're supposed to experience these places through you. They're not anymore. The ratings are slipping. I think maybe you need professional help before it's too late."

Shay shook her head. "The only kind of professional help I need is a nice quiet room in Arizona and lot of mental rest and relaxation."

"Bruce, Marvin and Leo. That's three guys in five years, and three relationships ending the same way. You need help. You need a therapist. You see women and couples on the happiest days of their lives, and you keep getting dumped. That's gotta affect you."

"It doesn't," she said emphatically, tossing her napkin on the table and motioning to the waiter to bring them the check.

"Then you are so in denial."

Shay rolled her eyes and shook her head. "It sounds like some of that psychobabble book speak is rubbing off on you. Why is it that every time a person disagrees with someone else it's called denial?"

"I'm not a therapist, I have no idea. But in this case it's true, you are."

"You know what?" Shay said, handing her credit card to the waiter. "The only thing that's affecting me is stress. I've been working nonstop for months, no, make that for years. Two and a half weeks away from the show and away from this drama, that's all I need," she said quickly, as she cut her eyes across the restaurant to Bruce and his fiancée. "And when I get back you can best believe *Romantic Destinations* is going to be better than ever."

"Now that's the spirit I want to hear. Oh, wait," Jade said suddenly, reaching into her large purse. "I have just the thing. Here, you need this more than I do right now." She pulled an invitation out of her purse and slid it across the table.

Shay picked it up and read the invite, then looked at her friend. "What am I supposed to do with this?"

"It's Dr. Love. Go check him out. Trust me, his books are incredible. Everybody reads them. The man knows what he's doing. He's been the guru of romance for the past eight years. If anyone can give you pointers on romance, he can. He specializes in sex, seduction, love, romance, dating and relationships. He teaches these incredible workshops that literally sell out in a matter of hours."

"Good for him, but no thanks. I can do this by myself. I don't need help. Besides, his books are the reason Bruce dumped me."

"Well, I still think you need to check him out. He's doing an invitation-only book signing this evening. I've read his books and listen to his show on satellite radio. He's incredible. He could definitely broaden your romantic horizons."

Shay shook her head as she slid the invitation back to her friend. "My romantic horizons will be just fine."

Jade smiled mischievously. "You know, what you really need is a good old-fashioned hot and sexy vacation fling."

"Is that your professional diagnosis, Dr. Jade?"

"It is and you should even write about it. That'll definitely spice up the online article you're gonna write. So how long has it been since you had any erotic entertainment—five, seven, ten months?"

"Jade," Shay declared as she looked around.

"Well, whatever it is, it's been too long. So I think it's

time. You're going on vacation. Find yourself a gorgeous hunk of man and get your romance groove on."

Shay laughed as she signed the credit card receipt. "Now that's the best advice I've heard all night. And that's exactly what I intend to do. No more doomed relationships for me. I'm free and I'm going to enjoy it."

"All right now, you go girl," Jade said, cheering her on.

"I'm going to find the first gorgeous man in town, get him back to my room and ride out the rest of the vacation in style."

They laughed riotously as they grabbed their things to leave.

The car suddenly jerked to a stop and the driver blew his horn. Shay refocused her attention instantly. She looked out the front window seeing that a young couple had just walked in front of the car. The driver looked up in the rearview mirror. "Sorry about that, ma'am. It gets really busy around here sometimes and people don't always watch where they're walking."

She nodded as her musings faded. That conversation was just about a week ago. Now, thankfully, she was a few thousand miles away and ready for two and a half weeks of nothing but rest and relaxation. She glanced out the front window. There was another rush of several women hurrying toward the resort. "Is the resort always like this?"

"Some days it's more popular than others. I guess

today is one of those days when it's really popular. There are also a few major conventions in the city and just about every hotel, resort and inn within a twenty-mile radius is booked solid. This is the beginning of the area's really busy season."

"I see," she said.

"But don't worry, I'll have you there safe and sound in a few minutes," he assured her.

She glanced out the side window and smiled, remembering the absurd conversation about Dr. Love. She didn't need a therapist, personally or professionally. She was fine. She wasn't cynical about love, she was realistic. The happily ever after fairy tale just didn't happen to real people. It never did. There was no love at first sight or instant attraction. There was just the feeling of need and want. And what a person did about it was up to them.

So right now, all she needed was a couple of weeks away to recharge. And what she wanted was a quick distraction from it all. The show was on a six-week hiatus and after months of continuous travel, she needed a mental and physical break. And since the goal was to get a producer's credit this season, she needed to be refreshed and ready to get back to work with a few dozen new and exciting show proposals.

So far, she didn't have a single idea of what to do or where to go. She looked up at Serenity Resort again considering the possibilities, then immediately rejected the thought. The owners had turned her down before and she'd certainly been in far more extravagant locations.

Hawaii, Aurora, Scott, Aspen, Napa and Lake Tahoe were her most recent show locales. Serenity was in the middle of nowhere, not exactly exotic and as far as she could see, its most redeeming quality so far was that it was a few thousand miles from New York and her ex.

The car turned wide along the circular path to pull up in front of the beautiful adobe-style resort. She looked up at the building. It was exactly as the online tour showed, an eclectic mix of Southwestern styled architecture set against the lavish setting of Arizona's Sonora Desert. She took a deep breath and then released it slowly, seeing the small sign out front. It read Serenity and included a brief definition below. Suddenly the idea of the next two and a half weeks made her smile. This was exactly what she needed.

She arrived in early evening as she usually did when she traveled. She always wanted her first view of a place to be in the evening, near sunset. It helped set the mood of the show. The car stopped. The driver looked up in the rearview mirror again. "We're here. I'll take care of your luggage," he said. She nodded, grabbed her purse, put on her sunglasses and got out of the car. The bellman greeted her then hurried over as the driver opened the car's trunk. She glanced around and walked away from the main entrance toward the edge of the driveway. She looked out across the desert to the city in the far distance and the mountain range beyond that. The near setting sun blazed the sky a fiery red reflecting a purple haze along the distant mountainous terrain. Fine, she yielded.

The scenic view was definitely breathtaking. Maybe this resort wasn't like all the rest.

A few minutes later she turned and headed inside. The modest entrance gave way to a large garden atrium-style lobby. It was a surprise she hadn't expected. The first thing she noticed was its stunning center showpiece, a modernized fountain which resembled a clear wall of water flowing down from just beneath the ceiling's skylight. Crystal clear sparkling water poured and flowed against dramatic lighting into a lavish fountain below. It was certainly an impressive entrance.

She imagined it was supposed to be serene, but not today. The gentle sound of running water was overshadowed by a constant buzz of excitement in the air as a number of groups of boisterous women and couples milled around both outside and inside the main lobby area. She looked around, getting her bearings, then continued to the reception area.

A petite woman looked up from the desk and smiled graciously. "Good evening, welcome to the Serenity Resort and Spa. If you're here for the book signing, it hasn't started yet. The conference is running a little long. As you can imagine, there are a lot of questions for the doctor."

"Actually, I'm checking in. I have a reservation. My name is Shay Daniels," she said, handing over her credit card.

"Oh, I beg your pardon, Ms. Daniels. I'll be happy to assist you in checking in. Please have a seat." She motioned to the seat across from her desk as she took the offered identification.

Shay sat down. "I'm here for two and a half weeks. You mentioned a conference," she queried, hoping it wasn't a stereotypical loud and rambunctious sales conference. "How long will it be going on?"

"Today is the last day of this particular conference, so most of the guests have already checked out. We do have another conference coming in tomorrow, but I'm sure your stay will be quiet and peaceful for the next two and a half weeks." The receptionist turned to her computer and began typing. She waited a moment then frowned. "Hmm, I don't seem to have you listed, Ms. Daniels. Might your reservation be under a different name?"

Shay grimaced. Bruce had initially set up the reservation, but when they broke up she asked him to remove his name. "Yes, you can try under Bruce Payne."

The receptionist typed again. After a few seconds she nodded slowly. "Okay, yes, Ms. Daniels, I did have a Bruce Payne reservation. It looks like you were scheduled under the private couple's romance package. But unfortunately the reservation was cancelled a few months ago."

"What, no. He was supposed to remove his name and keep mine for the reservation."

"I'm sorry. I don't have you listed and we're completely booked for the next week and beyond. I can certainly check area resorts or hotels for you, but everything is pretty much booked."

Shay just shook her head. She couldn't believe it. "Yes, would you please check any area hotels, at least for the night?"

"Yes, of course." She quickly began typing then stopped. "Oh wait, it looks like I do have something available on-site. One of our guests had an emergency and checked out an hour ago. The room is vacant, but there was only one night left on the reservation. I can give you that room for the evening and continue looking for something else in the area."

"Yes, that would be perfect," Shay said, relieved. At least she had a room for the night. Tomorrow was another story.

"The room is being cleaned up right now. It will be ready in another hour," the receptionist added.

Shay nodded.

"Can we expect Mr. Payne later this evening?"

"No, definitely not," she said assuredly.

The receptionist nodded without questioning. "Okay, you're all set. You're reserved in a guesthouse suite. It's a single suite located behind the hotel."

"That sounds perfect," Shay said, hoping for the calm the resort promised, at least for one night.

The receptionist continued typing, pressing one last key with added flourish. Afterward she looked up smiling as she returned the credit card and passport then gave Shay her room card. "You're all set, Ms. Daniels. I am sorry about the mix-up and I'll certainly continue to search the immediate area for alternate accommodation."

"I'd really appreciate that."

"It's my pleasure. I'm printing out some pertinent information to make your evening more enjoyable. Would you like me to have your luggage delivered directly to your suite as soon as it's available?"

"Yes, that would be perfect," Shay said, noticing a small group of women chatting excitedly as they hurriedly walked down the hall. "I think I'd like to look around first."

"Of course," she said, reaching over to the printer. "Here's a map of the grounds and directions to your suite. My name is Alona." She stood and reached out her hand to shake. "I'm with guest services. If you have any problems or questions, please ask for me. Also, please feel free to take a few minutes to look around the resort. We have several lovely restaurants on-site and a number of extraordinary guest amenities for your pleasure and enjoyment."

Shay nodded. "Thank you, Alona. I really appreciate all you've done. Tell me, if the conference is over and the next one hasn't started yet, why all the excitement this evening?"

Alona smiled. "Dr. Quinn Anderson is finishing the last day of his weekend conference with an open forum. Also, this is the last day of his national book signing tour."

"Dr. Quinn Anderson, as in Dr. Love," Shay said.

Alona, nodded. "Yes. He'll be signing books in a few minutes. The signing is open to the general public."

Shay immediately thought about her conversation with Jade the week before. She knew about the infamous Dr. Love of course—who didn't? His books sold millions and he was syndicated in some form in nearly every city in the U.S. He was a nationwide phenomenon and constantly growing in prestige. "Where exactly is the book signing?" Shay asked curiously.

"The signing will be in Serenity Salon A. There's a line forming along the far corridor. It's already pretty long. But since you're a guest of the resort…" she leaned closer and lowered her voice "…go along this walkway then make a left, then a right and then keep straight. You'll be at the rear of the conference area. As it lets out you'll be nearly first in line with the conference attendees."

"Thanks," Shay said, glancing down the walkway and nodding. Her writer's instinct immediately took over. She followed another group of women down the hall. They went straight, but she turned left and continued following Alona's directions.

Chapter 2

Quinn Anderson saw her as soon as she turned the corner. He glanced up, then did a double take and had yet to look away. She was stunning. Her smooth, flawless skin was the color of roasted pecans and her lips were full and sensuously enhanced with the slightest tint of subtle color. Her hair hit just below her shoulders and flowed in loose waves. Her body was sexy and slender, but not thin. The fitted top she wore accentuated her ample breasts and narrow waist as perfectly as her pants attested to long, luscious legs. She was definitely built to give a man a night's pleasure. He unconsciously licked his lips. Just the thought of her beneath him made his mouth water and sent instant shivers through his body.

It had been a long time since he reacted to someone so quickly. And even then, never like this.

He knew his reaction wasn't lust, or rather wasn't *just* lust. In his profession he knew the subtle and not-so-subtle differences. His immediate reaction was telling: sweaty palms, surge of desire and passion, physical arousal, accelerated heart beat and emotional yearning. It was a classic textbook scenario and according to everything he knew scientifically, was completely impossible. Still it was what he felt.

He had been waiting for his turn to go inside. Leaning back against the side panel, he was far enough out of sight to observe her at his leisure. She seemed to be in her late twenties or very early thirties and she was undoubtedly the most beautiful woman he'd seen in a long time. He feasted his eyes on her stunning features for a few more moments then had every intention of stepping out and making himself known. But he didn't, at least not yet.

She walked slowly, casually, as if she had all the time in the world. Quinn took a deep breath then exhaled slowly as an admiring glint sparked in his eyes. His body tightened again. He was riveted to every move she made as he watched her glide near then stop. She read the first book cover poster, smiled, then stopped at the second, third and fourth. The closer she got the more stunning she appeared. She was definitely a tourist, and she wasn't the kind of woman he'd easily forget if he'd seen her before.

When she got to the fifth poster, she was directly

across from him. She was so intent on reading each poster, she never saw him standing there. He looked down the full length of her body and shook his head, admiring. This was one woman he had to meet. He pushed away from the wall and slowly walked up behind her. She still hadn't noticed him. He heard her chuckle as she tilted her head, obviously reading the cover copy. "Okay, Dr. Love, so how do I seduce a complete stranger?" she said quietly, apparently thinking she was alone. He smiled and answered.

Shay followed Alona's simple directions: a left, a right and then keep straight. But instead of keeping straight she made another left seeing a large open area to the side. It was empty except for several book cover posters set up on easels beside a series of cloth-covered tables. They were lined up at attention like soldiers between each table. She speculated this must have been the registration area for the conference. She looked around quickly to make sure there was no one around. Then she walked the length of the area, stopping to read each poster in turn.

She shook her head after reading the first one and then stepped to the next one and continued on to the last. Then she looked down the line, reading each title in turn, *The Process of Romance, The Secrets of Sensuality, Unlocking Your Passion, Freeing Your Fantasies and finally, The Sensual Seduction*. Each was more outrageous than the last. The last one proclaimed to reveal the secrets of romance. She chuckled to herself at the absurdity of its claim. There were no secrets.

But these were the books that made Bruce dump her. In hindsight, she wasn't sure if she should thank the good doctor or not. Being dumped was hurtful, but having Bruce as a boyfriend wasn't exactly a laugh a minute. He was needy and immature. Not exactly qualities for a long lasting relationship. Why they had stayed together for so long was beyond her. Perhaps it was because she was away eighty percent of the time.

Her eyes narrowed as she squinted and tilted her head to read the last poster again. Maybe she should pick up a copy. Then she remembered Jade's suggestion of having a vacation affair with a stranger. She chuckled to herself, wondering if she could really do it. Why not? If they were strangers and neither gave their names, it might be fun and certainly an experience to remember. Besides that, she would be gone first thing in the morning and she'd never have to see her fantasy lover again.

Onc night only. The idea made her giggle. It was a sneaky, sexy, tempting thought. All she needed now was the perfect stranger and perhaps a few pointers. "Okay, Dr. Love, so how do I seduce a complete stranger?" she muttered rhetorically.

"You start by saying hi."

A deep, sexy voice had shattered the stilled silence and made her jump. Shay gasped and turned quickly. The instant she saw him her stomach dropped and her heart jumped twice in less than a second. She felt as if she'd just hit zero gravity. Her head seemed to spin and everything around her went hazy, except for him. He was brilliantly crystal clear. Everything else faded into the background.

A second later her heart sped up like a snare drum and she was sure she had stopped breathing. *Have mercy.* He was definitely the perfect stranger. He was over six feet tall, well built and too gorgeous. To call him eye candy was an understatement. She smiled. Yes indeed, he was exactly what she needed, the perfect stranger. "You scared me."

"Sorry."

"Hi," she said, as a million thoughts zipped through her mind. She could get right to the point and rip his clothes off right here, right now. She smiled at the scandalous thought, having more merit than not. She really was wanting.

"Hi," he answered.

Neither spoke for the next few seconds. They just stood looking at each other. She released a long, steady exhale, realizing she had forgotten to breathe again. Goose pimples rose on her skin as a very wicked, sexy smile graced his full lips. She knew exactly what he was thinking. She was thinking the same thing. She looked down, first to his broad shoulders, and then to his massive chest and narrow waist. "Are you here for the Dr. Love conference?" she finally asked, finding her voice.

"Yes, are you?" he asked.

"No, actually I was just curious."

"Have you read any of the books?" he added.

"No, I'm not a big fan of self-help books."

"I believe they're a bit more than just self-help."

"Really, then maybe I'll try one."

"This one is an excellent read," he said, glancing down at the cover to the fifth poster. "*The Sensual Seduction,*" he read the title then turned back to her. His eyes focused and penetrated deep into hers. "It explores the many masterful techniques of seduction while extrapolating specific details of the interaction."

She smiled wryly. It was pure psychobabble of course, but this time she didn't mind. Just watching his lips move was sending her body on a physical and emotional roller coaster. Usually more restrained, she found herself itching to touch him. Boldly, she did just that. She touched the side of his face. Just as she imagined, it was firm, strong and soft.

As her hand dropped slowly, he captured it, drawing her to take a step closer. They were standing toe-to-toe. She looked up into his eyes. Kissing him right now was tempting. But instead she smiled. She liked the idea of making him wait. "Really," she said instead.

He nodded slowly. "Maybe you can tell me about it over dinner."

"Are you asking me out?"

"Yes."

"Good, then yes, I'd like that," he said.

"Wait. Are you married, engaged or otherwise attached?"

"No."

She believed him and nodded. "Good."

They paused another few seconds before each stepped back. Then he glanced around her at the door behind the poster. "I need to go inside. Are you coming?"

She shook her head. "No, I don't think so. You enjoy."

Shay watched as he walked over to the door and grabbed the handle. Before pulling it open he turned back to her. "Perhaps we should introduce ourselves," he said.

She shook her head. "Not necessary. Why spoil all the fun?"

He smiled that sexy smile she saw earlier then nodded and stepped inside. A second later it hit her that she needed to find out where they would meet for dinner. She was just about to follow him inside when she heard someone call her name. "Ms. Daniels." She turned. It was Alona.

"There you are. I'm glad I caught up with you. Your room for the evening is ready. I've already had your luggage delivered. Also, I found an excellent hotel in the city of Tucson for you. It's only a few miles away. They had a last-minute cancellation, so I reserved the room for you. They're holding it, but we need to get back to them immediately. So if you'll come with me, we can complete the transaction."

"Great," Shay said, delighted to have found an alternate place so soon. She turned, noting that the stranger had gone inside and not come out. She turned again and followed Alona back to the reception desk.

It took a few minutes to complete the arrangements.

The hotel room was confirmed and Serenity would see that her luggage was delivered the next day. She thanked Alona and headed out. But instead of going to her suite, she went back to the open area to make dinner plans with her perfect stranger.

Then she heard joyous laughter coming from behind closed doors. She walked behind the table and quietly opened one of the salon doors and slipped inside. She wanted to know exactly who Dr. Love really was.

The tête-à-tête was nice. He was still smiling when he stepped inside. It was sexy, seductive, provocative and most certainly arousing. She had stimulated every nerve in his body. He was attracted to her the instant he saw her, then speaking with her confirmed everything else he needed to know at that point. She was intelligent, challenging and audacious, the perfect candidate. She could certainly hold her own. Unfortunately, he was so distracted by her touch that he'd lost his train of thought. It didn't occur to him until a minute after he walked inside that they hadn't firmed their dinner plans. He quickly stepped out again. But now it was too late. She was gone. He went back inside. It was time to go to work.

Chapter 3

As soon as Dr. Quinn Anderson was introduced and walked into the main room, the audience stood with joyous applause. He smiled and waved graciously as he headed to the front stage. He shook his manager's hand then waved again. Applause rang out louder as he attached the cordless microphone to his silk tie. It was always a pleasure being home and doing what he enjoyed.

He greeted the assembled attendees and thanked them for accepting the challenge he put before them that weekend. They applauded. He asked them to remember what they learned and take just a moment to open their minds to a new experience. They applauded again. He challenged them to go back to their loved ones and make them happy. This time the applause was overwhelming.

Twenty minutes later he was ending the three-day conference with his customary charm and charisma. He posed scenerios and answered questions. The forum was unscripted and customarily, very informal. He smiled graciously as he walked around the room, mingling with the forum attendees. He nodded when needed and smiled when necessary. He was a pro when it came to this. It was part promotion and part sales with a larger part being the astute knowledge of human psychology. He was an expert in the field, with sex, seduction and romance being his specific specialties.

It was an unlikely field of endeavor and one he had stumbled into completely by accident. But once in, he had excelled beyond his wildest dreams. His fame and popularity were unparallel. Women and men bought his books, attended his lectures and listened to his radio talk show. But it wasn't enough.

All this was fine, but this wasn't what he really wanted. He was once a serious scientist and a promising professional on his way to the top in his field. His research papers and scientific studies on human sexuality drew rave reviews from the psychology community and accolades from his peers. But that was before the fame started. Now people came in droves just to hear him talk about sex and seduction.

He didn't mind; it was all part of a larger picture. He enjoyed writing books that helped people with relationship issues. But what he was really doing was preparing a major case study entitled *The Anthropology of Love*. The basic thesis was simple: examine the process of falling in love up close and personal. He would be presenting his initial results at the National Psychology Conference in four weeks.

It was a project he'd been working on for well over a year. Everything was complete. He had his hypothetical premise, his suppositious data, his indisputable research from test subjects and his theoretical conclusion. Now he had the four-week break in his schedule to complete his project. The only thing missing was the perfect partner on which to test and examine his theories. Unfortunately, finding her wasn't as easy as he had initially anticipated.

His subject had to be extremely self-aware, detached emotionally from constraints of a relationship and able to submit to the process he had outlined. Whether she needed to be aware of the study was a nonissue. But the most vital criteria was that he had to feel an immediate physical and emotional attraction. In other words, he needed the perfect woman. So far no one even came close.

He knew he'd know her the instant he saw her. But so far he hadn't come across anyone who fit the criteria. Now he was running out of time and he needed someone fast.

He saw a woman stand and a forum assistant hurry over to hold the microphone for her. She leaned toward the mic, smiling giddily, and then asked her question. "Dr. Love, in your new seduction book you write about having sex in public places. Are you saying sex in public is okay?"

"Actually, my book doesn't say that at all. What it suggests is the possibility of 'romancing' in public places," he began, explaining slowly to clarify his stance. The last thing he needed was to be misquoted. And he didn't need another scandal. The one last year was certainly enough. "Don't be timid about public displays of affection. Hold hands when you walk. Men, touch the small of a woman's back. Women, touch your man's arm or face tenderly from time to time. There's nothing wrong with a little flirting and seduction in public. Remember show and tell. No matter where you are, show the person you're with that they are desired and adored. The smallest gesture can make the biggest difference. But please be mindful of location. Some areas aren't as accepting as others. The bottom line is use common sense."

Another question was asked. "Dr. Love, when is your next book being released and what will it be about?" she asked.

"I'm taking a short break from writing books right now." There was a very loud, very disappointed collective "Awww" as the audience began to mumble under their breaths. "I'm currently working on something very different. It's entitled *The Anthropology of Love*. There is no release date as of yet. It's not my traditional how-to, self-help guide. It's more of a specific case study centering on a single subject—falling in love." Oohs and ahhs filtered quickly throughout the room.

"Do you use volunteers for your research and where do I sign up?" someone from the audience asked. Everyone laughed.

Quinn smiled and chuckled. "I'm afraid that's going to have to remain confidential."

There was another collective sound of disappointment as another question was quickly asked. Quinn answered as he continued walking around the room. He stood in the back as a woman relayed what she'd learned and how it had positively affected her life. He listened while studying those around him. He knew instantly. No one here fit his subject parameters. Not like *her.*

Then, out of the corner of his eye he spotted her. She slipped into the room seemingly unnoticed, but he noticed. She looked around the room then turned her attention to the stage. She didn't see him.

As Shay had suspected, the room was packed to standing room only and then some. She quietly closed the door behind her and looked around. The buzz of excitement generated from every direction. There was a man standing on stage—Dr. Love she assumed. He looked very different in reality than in his press photos, but she surmised with retouching, he could be made to look like anyone he wanted. He was smiling as a woman stood talking about her personal experiences from reading the books and participating in a past conference.

She thanked Dr. Love for his assistance in rejuvenating her relationship with her husband, including the fact that they were now expecting their first child. When the woman finished the audience applauded her success. Shay turned her attention back to the man on stage, but he didn't respond. Someone from the audience did.

"Thank you. I appreciate the compliment, but you did all the work. I just reminded you what you already had together. The idea is to keep the passion growing in a relationship. Seduction, romance and fantasies don't end when you slip on the ring and say 'I do' or when you commit to another person. That's when the fun begins."

Shay whipped around quickly as she looked for the deep, masculine voice coming through the room's speakers. The almost familiar voice seemed to come from all directions, but she couldn't figure out who was speaking.

"Okay, we have time for just a few more questions," the man on stage said. He was obviously the moderator. Several women stood, one nearly jumping from her seat while waving her hand frantically. He pointed to her and she asked a question, then there was laughter, including *his* laughter over the microphone.

From the corner of her eye she spotted him, her perfect stranger. He had been walking around in the back of the room. There was no spotlight. Still he seemed to radiate an inner glow. Heads were turned, as every eye tracked his movements. Shay shook her head, only half mesmerized. She watched his slow steady stroll. He moved with the ease of a panther. He was masterful. It took less than a second to realize he was the man she was looking for.

He was definitely Dr. Love. Tall, dark and too damn handsome, the man looked more like a *GQ* cover model than a renowned relationship therapist. He was suave and elegant with the mark of polished sophistication. His face was clean-shaven, chiseled and angular. He had full sensuous lips and dark piercing eyes that seemed to observe the entire room in one easy sweep. He carried himself with ease, passing by women who, near swooning, frantically fanned themselves in his wake. She nodded. She could certainly see the appeal. He was gorgeous.

She suspected he knew his effect on others. He was too assured and confident not to. He smiled generously and she could swear she heard someone sigh. All eyes followed him as if mesmerized by his presence. Several more questions were asked, but Shay was no longer listening. Like the majority of the women there, she was too busy watching. But not him. She watched the women watching him. It was amazing.

He laughed. "Good question. To tell you the truth I have no idea why men lie. And to be fair, I have no idea why women lie, either. In some cases it's out of fear, in others, it's protection or desperation. What do you think?"

Shay nodded. Okay, he was good, she thought, still looking around the room seeing the enamored faces as a discussion ensued and he walked toward the middle of the room. No, he was way better than just good. He was exceptional. He had style, poise and of course he was breathtakingly handsome. Who cared what he was saying? Just looking at him was enough to set a woman's body on fire. He even had her believing his love and romance rhetoric—almost.

"...Well, as I said earlier, it's not rocket science. Making love comes from the heart, nowhere else. Men are just as afraid of being hurt and rejected as women." There was a spattering of disbelief. "I see I'll have to do another retreat for the few disbelievers." There was applause and more laughter. "No, I'm serious, think about it, what makes a man any different from a woman when it comes to getting hurt? Heartbreak is heartbreak. I certainly can attest to my share." There was serious incredulity at this point as rumbles of laughter and whispers of private conversations circled the room. He used this opportunity to get back to the stage and quickly speak to the moderator.

Shay nodded. She had to give him his Svengali props. The audience, made up mostly of drooling women, was enraptured. They seemed to worship every word from his mouth. When he smiled, she could actually hear the sighs around her. "Oh, you are good," Shay muttered to herself louder than she expected. "And I'd love to find out just how good you really are." The women standing near to her giggled, obviously agreeing wholeheartedly with her statement. He turned to the sound of laughter then continued talking.

"Making love doesn't come from a place of control or dominance, although each has a specific place in the process. But to answer your question, no, true sexual enjoyment comes from the pleasure of giving yourself willingly to your partner and vice versa. Think bold and be spontaneous… Step up and ask for what you want. How else are you going to get it?"

"Good Lord, can you imagine taking him to bed with you every night and asking for what you want?" the woman beside her whispered in a very pronounced Texas drawl.

Shay smiled. "Is that a conference option?" she asked jokingly. This time laughter was much louder around her. Quinn turned in her direction again then paused before continuing. No doubt about it, he had been looking directly at her.

"Remember the key words of romance. Target. Tempt. Touch. Tease. Taste. This conference focused on the romance of fantasy, making your desires known. So, let's wrap it up with a short exercise. Tell me your fantasy," he said, getting back to the podium. He looked around waiting for someone to answer. Obviously no one was bold enough. "Come on, somebody must have a fantasy. We just spent three days together outlining the possibilities," he said. There was shy laughter. "So, right now, this minute, tell me your fantasy. What do you want?"

Answers began being called out. He elaborated on each one, defining the clinical term, outlining the attributes and finally, sharing specific tips on making the fantasy become reality. There was a lingering snicker through the crowded room as slightly embarrassed couples and singles looked at each other and smiled. Some wrote feverishly while others nodded seeming to absorb every utterance. “Anyone else have a fantasy they wish to explore? Remember to be bold. If you can fantasize then you can make it real. Tell me what you want.”

Shay couldn’t help herself. The word left her mouth before she even realized she’d said it. The answer to his question was simple, “You.” Everyone turned around, looking for the person brave enough to say what the majority of the women in the room were thinking but were too shy to speak out loud. Shay didn’t reveal herself. She didn’t need to. Dr. Love was looking right at her when she answered.

“That’s very flattering, but…”

“But what?” she asked boldly, her voice deep and sexy. She took a step forward as everyone turned to see who spoke. The assistant with the microphone hurried over. “I’m only doing what you just suggested. Be bold and spontaneous, right?” Her brow rose for added emphasis. Heads turned back to him as if at a tennis match.

He smiled tensely, observing his pursuer. “Correct.”

“So, as per your instructions, the spontaneous me just boldly answered your question. What do I want? What’s my fantasy? Right now the answer is you.”

“Unfortunately, I’m not an attainable fantasy,” he said, taking a step forward.

“Why are you not an attainable fantasy?” she asked. “Correct me if I’m wrong, but isn’t everyone attainable to some degree? We just need to know the right buttons to push." Heads instantly turned in his direction for the answer.

He nodded, openly enjoying the scintillating banter. He also wondered just how far she'd take this. He decided to test her. "Psychology 101 assumptions aside, let's just say I'm an impractical fantasy at the moment. I would simply be sitting in for the man you really want to be with. That wouldn't be fair to either of us. Neither would ultimately enjoy the pleasure in the mutual outcome and we would want to enjoy the pleasure of the outcome, wouldn't we?" His voice trailed off softly as each word was slowly enunciated. There was no mistaking his meaning and intent. There was an excited muttering as all eyes shifted back to her in ardent anticipation.

She smiled. "Yes, definitely," she assured him.

"Therefore in essence I teach rather than participate."

"So in other words, some teach and write books because they can no longer participate."

The audience, hanging on every word, shifted their attention in anticipation of his reply. He smiled and chuckled silently as his jaw visibly tightened. "On the contrary," he began as a devilish grin appeared, "some teach, write books and participate extremely well. Some also see the thin professional line between them. I don't cross that line."

"What if there is no line?" she asked. Heads turned to him.

"Then I'd have to reassess my options." Heads turned to her.

She smiled mischievously. "Then by all means, reassess me."

All eyes shifted to him as his full sensuous lips turned up to smile. "Is that a proposition?" he asked. The inquisitive glint in his eyes sparked. All eyes turned to Shay. He watched as her chin stayed firm and even tipped slightly. He could almost see her calculating and hear her heart beating from across the room. She didn't reply right away. The room was deathly quiet.

"Consider it a reassessable option," she said.

"Then perhaps we should continue this discussion in private," he suggested seductively, one brow raised for added interest.

"Perhaps we should," she said.

The audience, witnessing the verbal seduction, made an "oooo" sound, denoting the new rush of excitement surging through the room. Shay nodded her assertion. Heads turned. He nodded as well. There was a moment of silence as everyone in the room seemed to be holding their collective breath, anxiously anticipating the next move.

The meeting of the minds was exciting. Quinn hadn't been drawn into such a lively and enjoyable one-on-one in a long time. Whoever she was, she was intelligent, poised, opinionated and quick. She had a witty, wry sense of humor and she kept him on his toes the whole time. He liked it.

A muttering of excitement sizzled all around them.

Everyone was talking and looking at her. Some proud, some envious and some still in shock. The moderator stepped forward, clearing his throat a couple of times. "Okay, after that I think we're gonna wrap this up right here." There was a collective "Awww" as everyone seemed to want to know what would happen next. "This seems like the perfect time to mention Dr. Anderson's newest release, *The Sensual Seduction*. I think by the last few minutes of this forum we can all attest it's definitely worth picking up.

"Also available today are *The Process of Romance, The Secrets of Sensuality, Unlocking Your Passion* and *Freeing Your Fantasies*. Thank you all for coming. The book signing will begin in about fifteen minutes. Have a safe journey home. Good night."

The applause for Dr. Love was nearly deafening. Shay smiled as she clapped as well. She had to hand it to him, he was impressive. But he was certainly not the great and powerful Dr. Love Jade proclaimed him to be. He was fallible, or at the very least, mortal. She made her point. Still, she admired his resolve. He was the perfect pitchman for romance.

Chapter 4

Quinn watched her from the stage as the program drew to an end. He wasn't sure what to make of her yet. That, in and of itself, interested him. He was always able to quickly ascertain a person's intention. He suspected she wanted something from him. They all did—why else would she even be there? The question was, what did she want? Whatever it was, and whoever she was, she played her part extremely well. She had audacity and she certainly gave as well as she took. Where most women were either too timid or in awe around him because of his perceived reputation, she certainly wasn't. She was the exact opposite. That intrigued him. She had an air of near scorn that bordered on impertinence. She'd all but publicly proclaimed her intentions in challenging him.

It had been a long time since someone had gotten to him. She had instantly. To most, he was Dr. Love, renowned relationship psychologist and beyond reproach. His reputation was solid and very well deserved. He was very good at what he did, and well respected both in and out of his professional and business communities. He just hoped Danny knew what he was doing when he set this up.

He waved, nodded and smiled in gratitude for the resounding applause. When the program ended, a few women rushed the stage to speak with him before the signing. As they talked he glanced around the emptying room. Unlike some who hurried out immediately to assure their place in the book signing line, she stood in the same spot as before. She spoke with a few women as they left the room. He knew she hadn't attended the conference the last three days. He would have noticed her. She definitely wasn't the kind of woman a man could easily miss.

She was casually dressed in tan slacks and a turquoise-colored top. She carried a jacket or coat over her arm and a small purse slung over her shoulder. She was attractive, very attractive, but in a girl-next-door kind of way. She was medium height, with large brown eyes that locked on target and held when she talked. She had smooth mocha skin and dark wavy hair. Then there was her voice. That's what really got his attention. It was deep, sexy and sultry with just enough edge to be provocative.

He answered a few more questions then looked up

seeing that she'd been watching him. Their eyes locked and held long enough for several women around him to turn in her direction. She nodded with a small knowing smile. He nodded as well. There was definitely an attraction between them. That part was undeniable.

"Ladies, excuse me. I'm afraid you're going to have to cut this short and excuse Dr. Anderson. He needs to get ready for the book signing," Danny Wilson said as he approached the small gathering.

"Sorry, ladies," Quinn said. "I'll see you at the table." There was a collective sigh as he stepped away.

Danny anxiously steered Quinn through another assembled crowd of fans to the small room behind stage set up as a waiting area before the book signing began. "Okay, you want to tell me what that was all about?" Quinn asked quietly.

"What was what about?" Danny asked.

"That seduction scene I just performed on stage," he said as he poured himself a glass of water and took a deep sip. "I know I said I wanted to make the conference memorable and get people talking. But you need to let me know when you're planning something like that in advance. I don't like the idea of being blindsided and set up like that."

"Whoa, that wasn't me. I thought it was you."

Quinn looked at him sternly. Danny had been his friend and manager for the past four years. They'd been through a lot together. He was brilliant when it came to business management and financial assessments. He was shrewd, astute and resourceful with just enough guile to make his abilities seem effortless. He was the perfect manager. Whatever he needed Danny took care of quickly and efficiently. He wanted a memorable forum and it certainly was. That's why he naturally assumed Danny had set it up. "You know me better than that," Quinn said.

Danny nodded his head knowingly. Having experienced the craziness of wayward publicity, fanatical fans and tabloid insanity the past few years, Quinn would have to had been completely nuts to put himself in that position again. "Okay, it wasn't you and it wasn't me. That means it had to be Nola. Come to think of it, it does sound like a publicity stunt. Still, you have to admit, it certainly was memorable. And you did tell her you wanted to up your profile at this conference, making it something to really talk about. I think you got your wish."

"Memorable—yes, something to talk about—yes, great, terrific. But I was thinking more on the lines of handing out some kind of signing favors, holding a raffle and giving away some books, not being openly propositioned by a conference attendee in the middle of a crowded room."

"What better way to sell your new book on seduction than to actually perform the perfect seduction in a public forum?"

"An effective seduction is between two people, not between two people in a crowded room."

"Well, it looked and sounded pretty effective to me. If I didn't know any better, I'd say you two were already together. But as long as she's not married like the last woman, we're fine," Danny said. "Damn, I can just see the repeating headlines on that one."

"Don't worry about the married part. She's not married."

"How do you know?" Danny asked. "No ring?"

"A married woman would have never answered the question I posed to the audience like that."

"Again, how do you know for sure?" Danny reiterated.

"I know," he said assuredly. "Do whatever research you can. I want to know everything there is to know about her by this evening. Including where she's staying."

He nodded. "I'll take care of it. First I think I need to have a talk with Nola, and then I want to find and speak with your new friend. If they're working together she should already have her background check done. If not, I'll at least introduce myself and get her name to start digging."

"Good idea," Quinn said, seeing his publicist, Nola Gilbert, hurrying into the small room. She looked around quickly then spotted them and rushed over.

"Quinn, that was incredible," Nola gushed, breathlessly excited as she approached. "I wish I had the test audience in there for that last part. Your numbers would have been through the roof. You could probably pick and choose your own reality show after that performance. If the applause in there is any indication, the results would be off the charts. Are you sure you don't want reality television?"

"Positive, no thanks," Quinn said, drawing a firm line. The last thing he wanted was cameras in his bedroom.

Nola shook her head sorrowfully. "You would be great," she said then nodded. "Okay, okay, then I guess we should probably get you out front. The ladies are excited and getting a bit overly anxious to meet you."
Quinn took another sip of water, set the glass down, straightened his tie and headed to the door.

"Oh, by the way," Nola added, "that last part was brilliant. Your book *The Sensual Seduction* is flying off the shelves out there after that little performance. Women are picking up three and four copies. I'm glad I ordered an additional fifty boxes, but that still might not be enough. Word of mouth is free publicity and you certainly have that now. Everybody's talking about that great onstage seduction and the website orders are going crazy. Talk about sexual chemistry. You two were setting that room on fire. Actually, the banter could have been spiced up a bit more, but we can work that out later. I'm thinking about a repeat performance on a larger scale, maybe on the set of a live talk show. So who is she, a model, an actress?"

"I have no idea," Quinn said. "Isn't she with you?"

"No. She's not with me." Nola looked to Danny. He shrugged and shook his head. "Wait, you didn't set this up, either?" Nola asked.

"No, and she didn't attend the conference," Danny said. "I would have noticed."

"Okay, I can work with this if it goes sideways. You were simply placating another aggressive and possibly obsessed fan. We can do a preemptive press release right now."

"Why don't you hold off on the defensive counter-attacks until we find out exactly who she is and what she wants?" Quinn suggested quietly, as he approached the table. Before starting to sign, he spared a quick glance around the crowded room. The one woman he was looking for was nowhere in sight. He sat down. Nola's assistant had the first book already open and waiting for his signature. The excited reader stood antsy, anticipating her coveted prize. Quinn greeted her and thanked her for coming as he signed her book. Afterward, the next reader eagerly stepped up. And so it began.

Chapter 5

Shay stood away from the crushing bombardment of Dr. Love's near rock star persona. The line, now insanely longer than before, extended down the walkway and wrapped around the corner and down the hall again. The women excitedly inched forward, each clamoring for his momentary undivided attention as he signed their mini-hoard of mind books. She considered buying a book for Jade, but then decided against it. Instead, she hovered to the side, enamored by the psychological study of his super-amped fame.

After staying inside and listening to several women talk about their thoughts on romance, Shay decided she'd had enough. She eased her way along the back wall away from the mass of excitement. That was when she saw him sitting at the table signing books. At one point she stopped and watched as he took a photo with a fan. The woman smiled wide. Dr. Love smiled generously, but it was obvious he wasn't feeling it. He glanced around then seemed to spot her in the crowd. His eyes narrowed then brightened.

A slow, wanting smile graced her full lips. There was no need for a woman to wonder what to do when she saw a man like that. It was all about instinct. The question then became what to do first. Should she kiss him, licking his tasty lips into submission or just dive right in, release his tie and peel back his shirt? Shay chuckled to herself as the thought rolled around in her mind much longer than she expected. But it was worth it. She pulled out her cell phone, snapped a photo as he looked right at her smiling. It was almost like he read her thoughts.

"Now he's what I call a reason for a fantasy," a woman said as she walked over and stood beside her. Shay remembered her from the forum earlier. They had stood near each other in the other room. Her Texas drawl was unmistakable. "Aren't you going to get a book signed?" she said.

"No, I don't think so," Shay answered, glancing down the long outrageous line.

"I saw you inside. Honey child, that was really bold what you did. Do you actually know him?"

"No, I don't," Shay said truthfully, sending the photo she'd just taken to Jade. "I took the photo for someone else. She'll get a kick out of it. She reads his books all the time."

"Really, and you don't know him. Hmm, I would have thought you knew each other for sure because y'all had some serious sensuous heat going on in there. I swear that room heated up twenty degrees. Oh, sorry, I didn't introduce myself, I'm Rose Kenner, Dallas, Texas."

"Hi, Rose. I'm Shay Daniels, New York."

"Nice to meet you, Shay," Rose said.

"Texas, huh?" Shay said with an easy smile. Rose's exaggerated Texas drawl was unmistakable.

"That's right, born and raised. I've lived there all my life. So, what do you do, Shay?" she asked curiously.

"I work for the Romance Channel. I write and host the show *Romantic Destinations*."

"Oh my goodness, I thought that was you. I love that show. Seriously, you must have the best job in the world. So, tell me, what's the inside scoop? Is your show coming here next season? That would be incredible."

"Actually, I'm just here on vacation right now," Shay said, looking around at the mass of excited smiling faces around them, "same as everyone else."

"Oh, honey child, please. Trust me, ain't nobody here just for vacation. They're here for one thing—him," Rose said as she glanced across the hall at the excited women in line. "Honey, if I knew it was that easy to get him all heated up like that, I would have spoken up myself years ago. Of course my husband would have had a fit." She winked, flashing a long curly fake eyelash. "Still, you certainly got his attention. And by the looks of it, you still have it." She nodded her head across the open area.

Shay turned, seeing Quinn looking right at her. "That's not exactly what I was going for. I was just curious about what he'd say when I responded with the obvious reply."

"You know you're the envy of damn near every woman here."

"Even you?" Shay asked, joking offhandedly.

"Hell, yeah, even me. I would love to have Dr. Quinn Anderson notice me like that. But I'm a realist. Also I'm sixteen years into a once fading marriage that's getting a whole lot spicier thanks to that man over there. He put the spark back in our romance. I can barely keep up. Who needs Viagra?" She laughed loudly and long. "All anyone needs is a little seduction."

"Is that why you just spent the past few days learning how to live out your romantic fantasies?"

Rose leaned closer. "Like you, honey, I crashed the party after the fact. I'm staying here at the resort. We checked in this afternoon. My husband is attending a conference this week and I decided to tag along and get my book signed."

"So you're a fan."

"Honey child, I'm a huge fan. What about you?"

"Let's just say I'm a curious observer at the moment. So, do you really think he's for real?"

Rose nodded and she looked over at the table again. "Hell yeah."

"Dr. Anderson is most definitely for real." The second

answer came unexpectedly. Both Shay and Rose turned. They hadn't noticed that a man had walked up and stood beside them. He extended his hand. "Good evening, ladies. I'm Danny Wilson."

They shook hands. "I'm Shay Daniels. This is Rose Kenner," she said. "You were the moderator, right?" He nodded. "So you know Dr. Love?"

"Actually his name is Dr. Quinn Anderson and yes, I know him. I'm his manager."

"I see. So this is all just a stage show, right?"

"If you've read any of Quinn's books, you'd know this isn't a stage show. He's genuine. He really helps people and enjoys doing it. Perhaps if you and your husband attend one of the seminars together…"

"I'm not married," Shay said, noting Danny's obvious relieved reaction.

"I see you don't already have Quinn's new release."

"No, I don't."

"Then perhaps you'd allow Quinn to gift you this copy. I'm sure he would be more than delighted to sign it for you," Danny said, handing her the book he'd been holding.

"Thank you," she said, taking the book and glancing to the waiting line. "I think I'll get this signed another time. The line is still a bit long."

"Are you staying here at the resort?" he asked.

"For one night, yes, I am, in one of the guesthouse suites."

"Perfect. I can have a book signed and delivered to your casita later this evening."

"Thank you. That's very generous."

"My pleasure," he said. "It was a great honor meeting you both. Thank you for coming. Enjoy the rest of your evening."

Shay looked at the book in her hand. "*The Sensual Seduction*," she said, reading the title aloud.

"It's really good," Rose attested. "He does a step-by-step process and teaches you to open yourself up to new experiences in romance, seduction, love and fantasies. It really changed my marriage." She glanced at her watch. "As a matter of fact I think I'm gonna get back up to my room and try out a new fantasy I read about in chapter fifteen, phone sex with hubby. He's in a meeting right now. What do you think?" She winked and giggled.

This time Shay joined her, imagining her husband getting phone sex while sitting in a crowed meeting room. "It was good meeting you, Shay. Maybe we can get together while you're here, or are you not alone?"

"I'm here alone, and getting together sounds like a great idea. Why don't we do that?"

"Super. You know I live right in Texas and I've never been to Tucson, so I signed up for a couple of city tours. Why don't you join me?"

"That sounds like fun."

"That's a bet," Rose said, agreeing happily. "What's your suite number?" she asked. Shay grabbed the key card from her purse and gave her the room number. "Great. I'll give you a call tomorrow. Right now I'm gonna head on up to make that phone call." She winked again. "We'll catch up later."

"Definitely, take care." As soon as Rose walked away, Shay's phone rang. It was Jade. She smiled and answered. "Hey, did you like the photo I sent you?"

"Three questions. Is this who I think it is, how'd you get the photo and forget the article, how long will it take you to get an interview with him?" Jade asked.

Shay laughed. "If you think it's your Dr. Love, then you're right. He just finished a seminar on romantic fantasies here at the resort where I'm staying. I'm standing here looking right at him," Shay said, turning. Quinn was busy talking and laughing with several enamored fans. "Girl, this whole sideshow is outrageous. It's like walking into a teenybopper worship-fest. The only thing missing are screaming fans, but I suspect it's about to happen in the next few minutes. So, do you want me to get you a signed book?"

"No, I want you to get me *him*," Jade said.

Shay chuckled. "Yeah, you and a few thousand other women here." They laughed. "Seriously this place is a zoo. I have a feeling it's only the beginning."

"Well, the man is insanely hot and gorgeous and rich and talented and he definitely knows how to move a woman."

"Please, it's all smoke and mirrors. He's just a regular guy with good PR."

"See, you are so cynical."

"If by cynical you mean intuitive, then you're right. I don't buy all his perfect romance stuff."

"You are impossible. But, you know, I was thinking.

Remember the other day when we ran into Bruce at the restaurant? We were talking about Dr. Love then."

"Yeah, what about it?"

"It's like the universe is talking to you or something. You're there and he's there."

"Yeah, so, what about it?" she repeated.

"You didn't want to go on this vacation, but you went anyway, and now you find out Dr. Love is there. Don't you find that extraordinary?"

"It's a coincidence."

"No, it's like the universe is talking to you. You're supposed to be there to talk to him so he can help you with your romance issues."

"I don't have romance issues," Shay said, looking around.

"He specializes in romance and relationships. It's perfect."

"No thanks. The last thing I need is an overrated shrink telling me I'm emotionally detached. And what exactly can he teach me that I don't already know?"

"He could help you loosen up. He could also soften your image for the camera and teach you about real romance," Jade said.

Shay just shook her head, watching him. "I bet he doesn't have a clue about women or what we really want and need."

"See, that's where you're wrong. He's a bestselling author, he does a satellite radio advice show and he even writes a syndicated newspaper column. The man knows women. He's brilliant when it comes to romance. His new book on seduction is incredible. I've actually tried some of his techniques and suggestions. They really do work."

"Good grief, don't tell me you've been brainwashed, too."

"Okay, okay, I get it. You don't want his help, so then how about getting an up close and personal interview with him. Our online readers would go crazy for that. We can do a whole week on him and then tie it in with the show's return next season."

"Actually that's a good idea."

"Also, I know for a fact that the network has been trying to get him for years. If you can land an interview, there's no way you won't get promoted to producer."

Shay considered it. "I'll see what I can do. I met his manager earlier. Maybe I can arrange something with him, but no promises."

"Great, still, if you ask me, the answer to what you need is staring you right in the face."

"Talk to you later." Shay closed her phone and turned. Dr. Love was busily signing a book while talking with a reader, nearly unaware of the constant barrage of clicking cameras around him. She watched. An instant later, as if he sensed her staring, he stopped and looked across the room right at her. Her stomach fluttered. *Have mercy.*

Chapter 6

Shay went to her suite and spent the rest of the evening researching and gathering as much information as she could on Quinn Anderson. If she was going to ask for an interview, she needed to know as much as she could about him.

Finding him online was easy enough. He was everywhere. There were hundreds of websites dedicated to him, his books, his lectures and his celebrity. She found that his credentials were impeccable and his professional background was even more impressive. He was born into a prominent, wealthy family. His father was an investment banker and his mother a college professor. His first book, written eight years ago, was based on his doctoral dissertation. It sold over a million copies in the first year. Since then his books had remained on bestseller lists for months.

Unfortunately, she also discovered getting an interview wasn't going to be as easy as she'd hoped. The last one was more than three years ago. It was right before he was involved in a major scandal. She remembered it well, but still looked it up online. A woman had filed a paternity suit against him and her estranged husband accused Quinn of committing adultery with his wife. It was later proven that not only wasn't he the child's father, but he had never met the woman. All charges were subsequently dropped. Apparently the woman had had an affair and decided to name Dr. Love as the baby's father. Since then there was nothing on Quinn other than his published books.

By now her curiosity had gotten the best of her. On paper it appeared his life was perfect, but Shay didn't buy it. She quickly realized what was missing—his personal life. Even before the scandal, there was very little published about his personal life. It seemed he guarded his privacy very closely. She wondered how a man who professed to be an expert on love, romance and relationships had no one in his life.

As she continued to probe, her cell phone beeped. She picked up the phone, opened it and saw Jade had sent her a text message. She read the message then answered.

Jade: I forgot to ask before, how's the vacation going?

Me: Stalled. I can only stay here at the resort for 1 night.

Jade: Why?

Me: Bruce cancelled everything. I should have checked and confirmed on my own. I guess I'm just so used to my assistant taking care of all my travel arrangements.

Jade: Bummer. What are you gonna do?

Me: They found me another room in Tucson—probably not as nice.

Jade: At least it's a room.

Me: True.

Jade: Have you come up with an approach for Dr. Love yet?

Me: No, nothing! How am I supposed to do this?

Jade: Don't know. I just read he doesn't do interviews anymore.

Me: Yeah, I just saw that too.

Jade: There was a bad experience after a scandal years ago.

Me: Swell, more good news <sarcasm>.

Jade: What can I do to help from this end?

Me: Send me a miracle.

Jade: (LOL) I'll look around and see if I have an extra one lying around.

Me: I don't even know if he's staying here at the resort or already checked out. The conference ended after the book signing this evening.

Jade: Then he's probably staying over.

Me: I'll find out tomorrow, so much for my nice restful vacation.

Jade: That's why it's called show business. Good luck!

Me: Thanks! I'll let you know what I find out later…

She ended the conversation thread and closed her cell. She started to go back to her internet search, but changed her mind. She wasn't getting any closer to coming up with a way to get an interview. She decided her best bet might be to ask Alona if it was possible to contact Danny Wilson. It was a long shot, but worth a try.

It was dark outside when she finally called it quits and looked up from her laptop. She was exhausted, but was too wound up to relax knowing sleep would elude her anyway. She never slept her first night on location. And tonight she knew it would be even worse.

Restless, she sat back and looked around the room. As promised, it was everything a luxury suite should be and more. Large and generously furnished, the chic rustic charm of the guesthouse was a pure Southwestern motif. It was stylish and sophisticated with an aura of historical authenticity. She got up, opened the sliding glass doors and then stepped out onto her balcony.

It was late, a little before midnight. The night was peaceful and there was a calm stillness hanging in the crisp cool air. Realizing she was hungry, she remembered seeing a quaint bodega-style restaurant in the lobby. She knew a full stomach and a walk in the night air would help relax her. She grabbed her jacket and key card, locked the door and headed out.

Her guesthouse suite was located at the far end of the resort property. It was surrounded by a tree-lined garden in a sea of brightly hued flowers whose faint floral fragrance drifted delicately on the evening breeze. She looked up. A billion stars sparkled brilliantly as the full moon shined down on her. The sensation was soothing. Everything seemed as if it had been suspended in time. She still couldn't believe she was here. This was the last place she expected to be right now.

Truth be told, she never even wanted to come in the first place. It was originally Bruce's idea. He'd set it up and then begged her to go with him. He seemed to think it would be good for them. She didn't buy it. As far as she was concerned their relationship was just fine as it was. They broke up a few weeks later. Apparently she'd been wrong.

Walking briskly, she headed along the brightly lit path she took earlier to get to her suite. It circled around the side of the main resort, past the pool, spa and fitness areas. She got to the main entrance and went inside, seeing that the restaurant she intended to go to was already closed. She walked over to the man standing at the reception desk. He looked up as she approached. "Good evening, my name is Carlos. May I help you?" he asked, smiling.

"Good evening, yes," she said, barely registering that he was the only person in sight. "My name is Shay Daniels and I'm in one of the guesthouse suites. Is there another restaurant around here still open?"

"Not on the premises. The two resort restaurants are closed for the evening. Room service is closed as well. There are several restaurants still open in town. May I call you a cab or have your car delivered?" he offered, reaching for the phone.

Shay looked around, considering her options. This certainly wasn't what she expected for her first night.

She quickly decided. "You know what, never mind. Thanks anyway." She took a step back to leave.

"Would you like to leave a breakfast request?" he asked.

"No thanks, good night."

"Good night, Ms. Daniels."

She turned and walked back outside, looking around the deserted driveway and parking lot. Instead of heading directly back to her suite, she walked across the driveway to the lookout point. She stood peering out beyond the stone barrier near the edge of the large driveway. Much of the panoramic view she'd seen earlier was obscured in darkness, but she did see the glittering lights in the far distance. It was Tucson.

Resembling a scatter of sparkling diamonds tossed across black velvet, the view was stunning. She wrapped her arms around her body, feeling a cool breeze blustering near. The stillness of the moment gave her pause. Maybe she had lost her center. Maybe it was time to stop and refocus. But she had no idea what to do next. How was she going to interview Dr. Love and possibly get him on the show? It was impossible. She stared out into the distance as if the answer was somehow hidden in the darkness. Soon she lost herself in the peaceful still serenity of the moment.

Thoughts of Dr. Love took center stage. She had answered his question and he had avoided a valid response. She wasn't really serious when she answered. But now the idea of him as her fantasy made her wonder what it would really be like to be with him. She considered a fantasy she'd always had, her and a complete stranger, stranded in the middle of nowhere with no one else in sight. They'd make passionate love beneath the stars. It was exciting and daring. Something she always wondered about doing. But there was no way she could do it. She wasn't bold enough. Still the fantasy's image made her smile, her and Dr. Love, her fantasy lover.

After the book signing, Quinn had a late dinner meeting with his staff then attended a private reception in Tucson with friends. Later he came back to the resort and went up to his office hoping to get some work done. But he didn't. He sat at his desk distracted. The woman at the conference and her comments stayed on his mind. She'd gotten to him. He picked up his cell and called his manager. Danny answered on the first ring. "Did you get anything on that woman tonight?" he asked.

"Where are you?" Danny asked.

"In the resort office. I'm heading home in a few."

"Okay, I'll call you back in five minutes. I have something coming in now. I want to cross-check and confirm."

Quinn closed his cell and tossed it on the desk. He looked up at the computer monitor. The word processing screen stared back at him. It was blank and ominous and he was frustrated and restless from staring at it all night. It had been over two months since he'd written a single coherent sentence.

He reached up and shut the computer down, removing his flash drive and closing the laptop's lid. He turned the lamp off on his oversized mahogany desk and looked around his office. It was big and elegantly furnished like everything else in his world. He had the best of everything. He had what was an enviable lifestyle. Since birth, all of his wants, needs and desires had been instantly tended to. He never wanted for anything, particularly female companionship.

Women constantly threw themselves at him. Some he let pass by; others he caught. Still, a select few he held on to for a short while. He was certainly no saint and he enjoyed the pleasure of a woman in his bed. But he was also vehemently explicitly clear that there was no lasting relationship potential. Some believed, others didn't at first but believed later.

With women he'd been teased, tempted and toyed with. All in hopes of securing that ever-elusive wedding ring. But it wasn't going to happen. Once was certainly enough. Lately he'd been abstaining from physical intimacy. It wasn't a conscious decision; it just happened. He hadn't found a woman who interested him, until today.

His last relationship was with a woman who turned out to not only be merely separated from her husband, but also trying to land him as a partner in a reality TV show she wanted to sell to the networks. She had a serious agenda. She wanted to be famous and he was her ticket to the top. He'd ended it quickly.

He stood, walked over to the large picture window

overlooking the beautifully manicured gardens below. The stair step plateau resort was designed to give every room an elaborate view of the city of Tucson, the Tucson Mountains or of the still lake below the mountain range. His office was located at the very top and afforded him a nearly exclusive view of everything around the resort for miles.

He rarely paused anymore to see the beauty of his surroundings, but tonight was different. He spared a moment to stand at the window and survey the ambiance. It was always a pleasure to be home, one he certainly didn't appreciate as much as he knew he should. He'd bought Serenity four years ago. It was a small, private, barely sustainable resort at the time, but he saw potential. He also saw healing. Something he definitely needed, but as of yet was unable to find.

He looked down into the night, seeing a solitary figure dressed in white casually walking in the garden. The area was safe enough, so that wasn't a concern, although he did wonder about that person out this late. It was odd, since most resort guests seldom ventured out after dark because of the chilly nights. His thoughts drifted back to the end program and the woman who'd answered his question.

He was attracted to her the instant he saw her. She was the one. Denying it was only prolonging the inevitable. They had fire and passion, even in a crowded room. He felt it and he knew she felt it, too. It was in her eyes. The last time he felt the intensity of desire was with his wife. Their whirlwind romance had consumed them.

She caught him off guard. Few people were able to do that. But it was her remark that had hit him hard. "Some teach because they can no longer do." It troubled him. She was more on target than anyone around him suspected. No one had even come close to the truth. He was hiding behind the facade of privilege and power. But she had somehow seen through him. He looked down at the gardens again. The figure in white was gone. He turned, picked up his phone and flash drive then grabbed his jacket. He needed to clear his head. It was time to leave.

Heading down to the lobby he refocused on his work. Just as he stepped through of the elevator doors his cell phone vibrated in his pocket. He pulled it out knowing only a very few people had his phone number and even fewer would call him this late at night. He saw the caller ID then answered. "Yeah."

"Her name is Shay Daniels," Danny began. "She's staying at the resort in guesthouse suite number two. She works for a cable network in New York."

"In TV, doing what?" he asked, instantly tensing, thinking he had to contend with another television wannabe trying to make a name for herself.

"She writes and hosts a cable television show called, *Romantic Destinations* on the Romance Network. It's not a bad show actually."

"I've never seen it."

"Doesn't matter now. It looks like the show's about to be cancelled. The ratings are good, but the network is struggling financially."

"What's she doing here?" Quinn asked, loosening his tie and waving at Carlos as he passed the reception desk.

"I don't know, but as far as I can tell, she's just on vacation."

"Is she alone?"

"The original reservation was under another name, Bruce Payne. I presume he's her ex."

"Why?"

"The original reservation was for one room, but he cancelled it a while back. She apparently didn't know until she arrived. Alona found her a room here for the night then she's staying elsewhere. She checked in alone."

"What else did you find out?"

Danny continued with a few more details, generally pertaining to her job and her educational background. Quinn stepped outside still listening intently to his friend's report. The cool crisp air immediately invigorated him. He stood at the entrance of the resort, listening closely. Then, looking around, a figure in the darkness got his attention. "That's it so far," Danny said, ending his report. "She looks harmless."

"It's the harmless ones that concern me most. See what else you can find out. Maybe she's freelancing."

"Okay, I'll call you tomorrow," Danny said. "How's the research coming?" he added before hanging up.

"About the same."

"Maybe you should consider Shay Daniels. You had serious chemistry and she certainly got your attention.

And you are running short on time. You have four weeks before the lecture."

"I know. And she is a possibility. I'll think about it. I'll talk to you tomorrow," Quinn said, then closed his cell and started walking to his car, but he slowed his gait slightly, glancing across once more at the figure still standing at lookout point. The person hadn't moved. He paused curiously. Like a ghost from the past, the solitude of the person standing there alone in near darkness brought back a memory he hadn't thought about in years. It used to be him at lookout point in the middle of the night. That's when he decided to walk over.

As he approached, the familiar silhouette of a woman's body and her perfectly rounded apple bottom kept his focus. She stood at the stone barrier, hands pressed securely atop the chest-high pilings. He watched as she peered over the wall into the darkness below then back out toward the glittering lights of Tucson. He stood a few feet behind her, observing her stillness. Seeing her standing there reminded him of his wife and the life he almost had.

He'd married right out of grad school and she'd died shortly afterward. Each day he was reminded of the loneliness he resolved himself to live with. He still blamed himself for her death. Had he been there when she needed him, she might still be alive. The pain and guilt of that knowledge would be forever scarred in his heart. There was no way to move on. So he resolved himself to helping others find and keep love and not make the same mistake he did.

As he neared, he expected the woman to turn around. When she didn't, he moved closer, barely seeing her face in profile. Classic and serene, she was fully enamored, lost in silent meditation. Even though it was dark, he could tell her eyes were intent and focused in the far distance. He wondered what she was thinking. Then he turned to look out at the view he so often took for granted. To visitors and guests of the area, he could easily see how it would appear mesmerizing. "It's a little late to be out sightseeing, isn't it?" he said, looking out at the bright lights of Tucson.

Chapter 7

It was déjà vu all over again as Shay yelped, flinched and whipped around, obviously startled by the unexpected intrusion. "Are you nuts, sneaking up on me like that?" she stammered breathlessly, holding her hand to her chest, sparing a quick glance in his direction before looking away to get herself together. "What is with this place? Does everybody sneak around scaring people? You nearly scared me to death."

He took a cautious step closer. "I'm sorry, I didn't mean to startle you," he said. "Are you okay? Can I call someone for you?"

She shook her head. "No, I'm okay, I'm fine. You're lucky I didn't have my pepper spray on me or you'd be one…" she threatened, and then turned to look up at her intruder. She expected to see the man from the reception desk or a security guard, but it wasn't. It was him. The man she'd been reading about all evening and thinking about all night. "Dr. Love," she said, obviously recovering quickly. "You seriously need to stop doing that."

Seeing her and realizing who she was, Quinn's jaw dropped just seconds before he regained his composure. "You again," he said, seeing that she was equally surprised to see him standing there.

She nodded. "Yeah, me again."

"Actually it's Quinn—Quinn Anderson. And you are?" he prompted, extending his hand to shake while waiting for her to tell him her name.

"Shay Daniels," she said, grasping his hand firmly. "Looks like we meet at last, Dr. Anderson."

"Ms. Daniels," he said tensely as a muscle pulled tight in his jaw and he held her hand securely. "That was quite a performance you put on earlier this evening. Are you always that bold or should I be honored to be the exception to the rule?"

She smiled. "Be honored, although I do have a tendency to be overly inquisitive. Actually, I was curious as to what you'd say when I answered your question with what was on the minds of just about every woman in the room."

"Including you?" he asked.

"I said just about every woman."

"Including you?" he repeated the question.

"I hope I didn't embarrass you too much." She smiled, not answering his question for the second time.

"Not at all. It was a very stimulating exchange."

"Stimulating exchange, huh?" she smirked. "That sounds a lot like psychobabble speak for, 'I'd prefer you not do that again.'"

He half smiled. "You translate psychobabble very well," he said.

"I've had plenty of practice. My ex-boyfriend considers himself an amateur therapist."

"Ahh, I see," he said, nodding his understanding of a fact from Danny's report. He also quickly speculated her overly aggressive comments to be a case of simple transference.

"What do you see?" she asked suspiciously, knowing from experience the comment was either a tool to gain more insight or he'd just thought he figured her out.

"Well, given your ex-boyfriend's lack of credentials and the fact that he's your ex, I'd say you were exhorting aggressive behavior toward all therapists for lack of a tangible emotional release."

"Yeah, like I said, psychobabble speak for, 'I'd prefer you not do that again,'" she restated jokingly. He smiled, taken off guard by her candor. Their eyes connected and held for a moment. There was a comfortable silence as each seemed to openly assess the other. "I looked through your book on seduction earlier."

"Really, what do you think?" he asked, as he relaxed back against the stone wall. He expected to hear the usual favorable accolades.

"It was interesting," she said dispassionately, "but you seem to assume a lot. Like that most people know what they're doing when they try to seduce someone. I don't think that's particularly true. Not all people have the ability and I don't think it can be taught as easily as you prescribe."

"I disagree. The ability to seduce is an innate quality we all possess. We chase, we tease, we retreat, we pursue again. It's all about want, temptation and desire. We become, for lack of a better description, intoxicated when we seduce. Dopamine and pheromones are released and stimulated as the euphoria begins."

"What if we don't have that quality and the chemical makeup just isn't there?" she asked.

"With the right man and the right woman, trust me, it's there. It may be latent or suppressed by other defenses, but it's definitely there," he said assuredly. "That's why the conference was all about understanding desires and fantasies. Seduction is about playing through a fantasy role with a partner. It opens a doorway, giving the other person the opportunity to choose to walk through. You did that this afternoon."

"No way," she said, shaking her head steadily. "That was just me answering your question to see what you'd say. There was nothing remotely seductive about it."

He smiled wide. "Then you're better at seduction than you think. You accomplished the four main postures of an effective seduction. You got my attention. You piqued my interest, you challenged me physically and emotionally and finally, you left an opening for me to respond."

She shook her head as he spoke. "I don't know how you got all that from a three-minute back-and-forth conversation. I was just responding to your invitation."

"Seductions work when done back-and-forth."

"Fine, but believe me, that certainly wasn't my intent."

"Perhaps it wasn't your conscious intent," he suggested.

"Conscious or subconscious, it wasn't my intent," she reiterated.

"Are you sure?" he asked.

"I see you like to twist words around to support your theories. So whatever I say or do, it's solely a matter of your interpretation."

"There is no need to interpret anything in this instance. Your actions and your comments are indisputable."

"That's another presumed interpretation," she said.

He smiled knowingly. "Now you're just in denial."

She opened her mouth in shock then laughed. "I cannot believe you just said that. First of all, I am not in denial. And secondly, using 'denial' is the classic fallback bastion for everything anybody says to disagree with you head doctors."

It was his turn to laugh. "How do you figure that?" he asked.

"Don't tell me you disagree with me."

"Of course I do," he insisted.

She smiled victoriously. "Then that would mean you're in denial, wouldn't it."

He laughed loud and long this time. She smiled, observing his seemingly uncharacteristic humor. This wasn't the man she expected to find. And certainly not the man reputed as Dr. Love, a name with its own notable inferences attached. "You're a lot different than I expected."

"What did you expect?" he asked. She looked at him, deciding if he was capable of accepting the truth. "Come on, I can take it."

"I assumed you were either a player out to score as much as you can before the house of cards collapsed in on you, or you were an arrogant brainiac with a textbook stuck up your butt or…"

Quinn had been chuckling as she spoke, then he stopped, wondering what her third assumption might be. "Or…" he prompted, surprised that he was actually very interested in what she thought of him.

"Or, you were someone who was hiding, atoning for something."

He smiled tightly. She had hit the nail on the head and she didn't even know it. "I'm almost afraid to even ask what you decided."

She purposely didn't respond. She wasn't sure she knew. She turned away, looking out toward Tucson. "So, Doctor, how do you come up with your theories and conclusions? Do you ever field test your suppositions or just assume you're always right and that they'll work on the masses?"

"I do clinical research, subject studies," he said.

She turned back to face him. "Subject studies on seduction. Now how in the world does that work? Do you use volunteers or hire partners?" she asked suggestively.

"I interview test subjects," he said, then decided to clarify more. "I choose a number of acceptable candidates and work with them through a process."

"Do they know what you're doing?"

"Yes, they know. My studies are very systematic."

"You make it sound so clinical, like a science project."

He nodded his agreement. "To me it is."

"And the human factor?" she asked.

"Is always considered," he replied quickly, without missing a single beat.

She shook her head. "How can that possibly work? There are too many variables, personalities, backgrounds. We're all so different."

"Actually, we're not all that different. At any given time any woman can get any man she wants and any man can get any woman he wants. All they have to do is learn how."

"So if I read your book, I can get any man I want."

"As long as the other person is open and receptive, yes, my book will certainly get you started on the path," he said. He watched as she shook her head slowly. She obviously didn't believe him. "You don't look convinced," he said.

"I'm not saying you don't know what you're

doing. You probably do to some extent," she needled intentionally. His brow rose with interest. "I guess I'm just a little cynical. To tell you the truth, I think the whole romance thing is completely overrated anyway. It's all propaganda, Hollywood smoke and mirrors to see a dream and a fantasy. No one sees fireworks when they kiss and when was the last time you experienced a mind-blowing, toe-curling orgasm when you made love. Everyone expects so much from romance and when the expectations aren't fulfilled, they're either heartbroken or they walk out. And as for seduction, I think it's all in the mind. Not everybody is good at it or can do it. And a few books aren't going to change anything."

"You're right. Seduction is all in the mind. But it's also about confidence. It doesn't matter what you look like. It doesn't matter how much money you have in the bank. If you have the unflinching confidence that you deserve this happiness, then seduction becomes just another tool."

"You make it sound so easy," she said.

"Not at all. Romance, seduction, love—it's a lot of work if you want to succeed and be happy." She shook her head again. "Still not buying it, I see?" he offered.

"It's nothing personal, Doc. I guess I've just been too close to the game, that's all. I've seen too many people hurt in the name of love and romance."

"What game is that?"

"The romance game," she said.

"Meaning?" he asked confused, but interested.

"Meaning it's getting late and I think I need to raid a vending machine before heading back to my suite."

He looked at her, confused. "Vending machines? There are no vending machines here. Are you hungry?" he asked.

"Starved," she said. "I missed lunch and dinner and the restaurants here at the resort are both closed and it's a little too late to wander around Tucson looking for something to eat."

"Come with me," he said, turning to walk away. He wasn't ready to have this conversation end just yet. He was enjoying himself too much.

She didn't move. "Come with you where?" she asked.

"To get you something to eat," he tossed over his shoulder and kept walking.

She hurried to catch up, following him back into the resort. "Okay, so where are we going?" she asked. "By the way, room service is also closed."

"Wait here," he said, then walked over to the front desk and spoke to Carlos a few minutes. She watched as Carlos nodded several times, picked up the phone and made a call then shook his head. Quinn walked back over to her.

"No luck, huh? That's okay."

"The resort chef just left, so it looks like we're on our own. But I'm sure we can find something to eat upstairs. Come on," he said, guiding her toward the bank of elevators.

"What's upstairs?" she asked.

"The penthouse. The refrigerator usually has a little something in it, although I haven't been around for a while, so I doubt it's been completely stocked recently."

"How do you have access to the penthouse?" she asked.

"Owning the place does have its perks from time to time."

"You own Serenity." The elevator doors parted and they stepped inside. He pushed a button to the top floor then pulled out a key card and inserted it into a slot. The elevator moved quickly and quietly.

"Yes, I came here years ago to get away for a while. It was serene and peaceful. It was perfect. I bought it a few months later."

"And you live here?" she asked.

"No, not all the time, but for right now I do."

"I travel constantly and stay in some of the most luxurious resorts in the world. They're breathtaking. Still, I can't imagine living in one all the time."

"You get used to it." The elevator beeped and the doors opened wide.

Chapter 8

Quinn walked out into the open space and waited for her. Shay stepped out and looked around, seeing a beautiful apartment exquisitely decorated. But it was much more than just an apartment. It was two floors of architectural magnificence. Divided in two, the right side was set up like a den with comfortable seating, a marble fireplace and mantel, large flat screen television and two large corner curio cabinets. The other side had a small conference table with matching desk, credenza and stacked bookcases. Directly ahead were French doors and a wall of windows covered by thin sheers. She could see another low-lit room beyond that. Connecting the two sides were lush plants and oversized trees. Dim recessed lighting illuminated the rooms, giving them all a cozy, welcoming feel.

She walked in, stood and looked around. "You're right. This is definitely a perk." Black marble floor, mahogany wood, crystal chandeliers, Tiffany-style side lamps and plush furniture. She walked to the left and looked around, touching the conference table. "This is your apartment. It's beautiful."

"Actually it's my office and my apartment. There are three bedrooms and sitting rooms upstairs to the right. I don't stay here often, but sometimes." He took a few steps back. "The kitchen is this way," he said, turning to the left and walking down a short hallway. She followed. "I don't know what I have in the cabinets or refrigerator, but I'm sure between the two of us we can come up with something. What do you have a taste for?" he asked, as they entered the brightly lit kitchen. He went over to the main section and started opening all the cabinet doors and looking inside for rations.

"Chili, really meaty, crazy hot and super spicy," she said, following him into the small but nicely designed space. He stopped, turned then looked at her half smiling. "What? You asked," she said evenly.

"I don't think I'll be able to accommodate you with that particular request, but I'm sure there's something around here to eat." He pulled out a box of gourmet crackers and a small tin of caviar. "Here, this should get you started." He sat them on the center counter in front of her and continued looking around.

Shay picked up and opened the box of crackers,

pulled one out then took a bite. "Umm yummy, that's the best cracker I've ever had." She picked up the small tin of caviar and read the lid. "Almas caviar," she said and then grimaced, making a face, "Yuck." She sat down watching Quinn as he closed the cabinets then went to the refrigerator. He opened it, leaned in then shook his head. "Okay, we have a bottle of champagne, butter, fruit and cheese."

"Fruit and cheese sounds perfect, much better than vending machine pretzels and chips."

"Wait, I just found some eggs. Scrambled okay with you?"

"Yes, perfect. How about some help?" she said then removed her jacket and went over to the counter beside the stove. "Why don't you take care of the cheese and fruit while I cook the eggs?" she said.

"Sounds like a plan," he said, pulling out a small frying pan, a bowl and a whisk and setting them in front of her. She washed her hands then broke the four eggs into the bowl and whisked them with salt and pepper while the buttered pan heated up on the stove. He handed her the bowl and she poured the mixture into the pan. The eggs began cooking slowly. She turned and looked at him. He was watching her.

"Hey, aren't you supposed to be getting the cheese and fruit together?"

He nodded then went back to the refrigerator and pulled out the cheese and fruit. He grabbed a platter and glasses then opened the champagne and put everything on a tray.

"They're almost done. I need some plates," she said.

He pulled two plates out and placed them on the counter beside the stove. "I'll set this up in the other room." He picked up the tray and headed back down the hallway into the open space and then out onto the enclosed balcony beyond. He turned on music and was lighting the outside fireplace when she walked in.

"Wow, this is a serious perk," Shay said, looking around in awe.

He met her at the entrance, took the plates and sat them on the small table. She walked to the balcony's edge and looked out. She shook her head in wonder. "This view is incredible. How do you ever get anything done?"

"With great difficulty sometimes," he confessed.

"I bet." She turned. He was right behind her. "You know, I didn't realize this place was going to be this secluded and deserted at night."

"That's the whole idea of Serenity. Solitude, peace and tranquility," he said, looking around approvingly. "This is the perfect place to come when there's no place else to go." He spoke from experience. He turned back, his eyes locked with hers and held again.

"Is that the resort's slogan?" she asked after a brief pause.

He half smiled. "No, I don't think the resort has one."

"Maybe you should use it. It fits."

"Perhaps I will," he said, nodding, watching as she turned and looked into the darkness again.

"The view is exquisite," she said after another brief silence. "But it's a little too quiet for me."

"Serenity is more for reflection and tranquility. Are you looking for excitement?" he asked.

"Are you offering excitement?" she answered.

"I think you know a lot more about seduction than you think you do. Your trigger is wit. You tease and joke when you seduce. Then the question becomes, will you step up to the plate?"

"So you're saying humor is my defense."

"Yes, in a manner of speaking."

"You got all that from one conversation."

"Three conversations," he corrected. "The second was in front of a few hundred people. The first was alone in the hall outside of the forum room."

She leaned back on the iron rail. "Who could forget that?"

"Certainly not me," he said. The moment was quiet and intimate. He stepped closer. They looked into each other's eyes. He reached up and seductively ran his finger along the underside of her jaw. The slow delicate stroke set her body on fire. It was just enough.

He stepped back. "Come have a seat." She followed and sat down, taking a long deep breath. After he sat across from her, she looked over the spread they had prepared.

"Not too shabby for a midnight snack."

He raised his glass to toast her. "To midnight snacks," he said. She smiled and held her glass. Their glasses touched gently and then they each took a small sip before starting to eat.

"Umm, this is delicious," she said.

"It's not exactly the Essex House or Masa at the Time Warner Center," he said.

"I hear both are totally overrated," she quipped.

He chuckled softly. "You have a great sense of humor."

"Thanks, I get that a lot."

"You know it really is a defense mechanism."

"Isn't everything?" she said.

He chuckled again as they ate and continued talking casually about his books and his recent book tour. Then he changed the subject to her. "So tell me, what brings you here to Serenity, Shay? You obviously didn't come for the conference."

"My ex suggested it a year ago. He really wanted to meet you. He has all your books and lecture CDs. It was supposed to renew our relationship. As you can see, it didn't quite happen like that. So, since I thought the reservation was already made, I decided to come alone."

"I'm glad it didn't work out," he said.

"Really?" she asked.

He nodded. "Sure, if he had come, you wouldn't be here with me. How long has it been since you and your friend broke up?"

"Over six months ago, but it has been a bit longer since I travel a lot with my job. We were together for three years."

"It was serious then?" he questioned.

"He told me I was emotionally detached."

"Are you?"

"To him, probably," she said. "What about you? I read your wife died a while ago." He nodded. "I'm sorry." He nodded again. "Has there been anyone else since then?"

"No, not seriously," he said.

"Why not?" she asked curiously.

"Good question. I've been wondering that myself lately."

She wasn't sure what that meant, but she knew it implied something. "You answer questions, but you never quite say what you feel, do you?"

"Is that what you think?"

She nodded. "I'm beginning to get that impression."

"What questions do you have that you'd like me to answer?"

"Okay, an easy one. What's the definition of love?"

He laughed instantly. "I see you don't ask the simple questions, do you?"

"I know it's more than lust and the desire for sex, right?"

"Right," he agreed.

"So what is it exactly? I mean aside from all the fairy-tale nonsense we all grew up with."

"Well, some say it's a profound affection for someone else. It's physical, emotional and spiritual. Also it's the comfort of knowing and trusting the person you're with. It's at times being able to be completely free and honest to be yourself. That's a hard thing to do for most people. Opening up to touch and be touched. Others say love is knowing and showing one's vulnerabilities and feeling safe that someone won't take advantage of them."

"And what do you say it is?" she asked more specifically.

"There's no single definition, not even for me. But to give you an answer, I think it's the joining of spirits and a feeling of complete connection to another person. It's an attraction that goes far beyond the main senses of what we see, hear and feel. It's another sense all together. It doesn't matter about length of time or how long you've been together. The initial feeling can be instant and immediate and last forever or it can grow and thrive and take a lifetime.

"It's when you willingly give your heart openly without reservation. Simply put, love is the beginning of life. It's a giving and connecting of mind, body, soul and spirit. It can't be forced and when it's natural, it's the most incredible feeling in the world. It's passion that simmers and it's romance that explodes. Bottom line, the true definition is always best when it's experienced."

She took a deep breath, savoring his words. "Wow, that's a lot."

"Actually, that's not even close to the tip of the iceberg."

"Don't you ever get jaded by all this?"

"By romance, love, seduction?" he asked. She nodded. "No. Never."

"My friend says I lost my romance center."

"Have you?"

"I don't know, maybe. I'm not even sure I even had one in the first place."

"Shay, there's no secret to romance and seduction. It's all around us all the time. You just need to know how to focus on letting go and trusting what you feel."

"That's easy for you to say. You know all this. I don't have a clue how to seduce and romance a man. I've been dumped three times in the past five years. They all basically said the same thing, I'm emotionally detached."

"I find that hard to believe," he said. "You have so much passion and joy."

"Not according to them. I think I'm seriously doing something wrong. For instance, look at us here right now. This place couldn't be any more romantic, right? You have the soft music, the fireplace, champagne, caviar. The view is stunning and there's a million stars shining down on us. We're surrounded by every romance cliché in the book and there's nothing."

He stood and walked to her chair. "Stand up," he said softly, holding his hand out to her. She grasped his hand and he drew her up close to his body. He released her hand then reached up and touched her shoulders, running his hands down her arms. Her body willingly stepped closer. He leaned down to tuck his face into the sweet soft curve of her neck. His lips were just inches from her skin. "Tell me what you feel right now," he whispered.

Shay's body had all of a sudden melted from the

inside out. "I feel warmth, your breath on my neck," she confessed.

"Good. Is your heart beating faster, palms sweating, stomach fluttering?" She nodded slowly. He closed his eyes and leaned in closer inhaling deep. "Mine, too." Then he leaned back, seemingly unaffected by the moment. "That's seduction, and you responded perfectly," he said. "Romance is the action that got us to that point." He released her and on near wobbling legs, she sat back down. "What if I said I could help you, teach you. Would you be interested?" he asked.

"Help me, what do you mean?" she asked, still feeling the effects of his seduction.

"Finding your romance center again," he said. "I'll teach you what romance is and the seduction process to get you what you want."

"Why would you want to do that?"

"Because it's what I do. I try to help people."

"And what do you get in return?"

"Possible research. I'm always interested in developing new techniques in seduction and…"

"…And you want me to be your test dummy?"

He chuckled. "Hopefully nothing as drastic as that, but something on that line, yes," he said.

"Okay, but why me?" she asked. "Do you know how many women would love for you to make them this same offer?"

He smiled and nodded. "Yes, I'm well aware of the number of woman interesting in my research, so to speak. But I'd like someone less eager."

"You mean someone emotionally detached."

"I mean someone more likely to respond to my suggestions honestly and without preconceived notions. I think you can do that."

She bit at her lower lip again as she pondered his proposal. "I don't know," she said, shaking her head. This was just too good to be true. But then again, she was a New Yorker. When something seemed too good to be true, it probably was. But still, this was a golden opportunity. How could she pass it up? Learning seduction techniques and romance from Dr. Love would be incredible. If he was indeed everything they say. She'd have a great article and a possible promotion. But still…"Maybe, what do I have to do?" she asked.

"Nothing much. I'll make some suggestions, ask a few questions, you answer, I'll observe your response to varied stimuli and we'll take it from there."

"That's a lot of nothing much."

"Just be open to the experience. I'll help and guide you through the process."

"How long will this tutoring take. I'm only in the area for two and a half weeks, but I'll only be here at the resort tonight. I'm moving to a hotel in Tucson tomorrow."

"Don't worry about your accommodations. I'll make sure they're taken care of. As a matter of fact, perhaps you should move in here."

"With you?"

"I don't actually live here. I just stay here from time to time," he assured her.

"Why does this feel like I'm about to make a down payment on the Brooklyn Bridge?" she asked.

He laughed. "I assure you, the Brooklyn Bridge is not for sale, particularly in this case."

"I'll think about it."

He nodded. The meal ended and they continued to talk. But Quinn's proposition stayed on her mind. She couldn't believe he'd make her such an incredible offer. He was a master at seduction and romance. Who better to teach her, and what an incredible hook for her possible interview?

It wasn't until Quinn refilled their glasses for the last time that she noticed how late it was getting. They had been talking for over two hours.

"You must be exhausted after the conference and book signing."

"I'm fine. I've been enjoying myself," he said graciously.

"Thank you for this."

"You're very welcome."

"Can I help you clean up?"

"No, don't worry about it. The penthouse has a separate staff, valet, cook and housekeeping. You won't always see them, but they're around."

"I really enjoyed myself tonight."

"Me, too."

"Well, I guess I'd better go." She eased her chair back and he quickly came around to help. Then they stood in silence, facing each other. He reached up and gently stroked the side of her face. She closed her eyes, enjoying his gentle touch. The feel of his hand on her skin began to scramble her senses. She inhaled deeply, smelling the spicy undertone of his cologne and clean masculinity. When she opened her eyes he was staring down at her. "Um, if you're going to kiss me, this would be the time to do it," she whispered jokingly.

He smiled. "Really, thanks for the heads-up." Then he leaned down and kissed her sweetly. It was perfectly tender and chaste. A few seconds later he leaned back and looked at her.

"Okay," she said, hoping not to sound as disappointed as she felt. She expected more, after all this was the infamous Dr. Love. "I'm going now." She turned to leave then felt his hand on her arm. Just as she looked down, he pulled her back into his arms flush against his body. The quick action nearly took her breath away. She watched a muscle in his jaw tense and his eyes narrow. She knew want and desire when she saw it. Seeing his passion made her stomach flinch and her heart palpitate. A fast-moving current shot through her body, electrifying her nerves. In an instant he recaptured her mouth and this kiss was nothing like the last one. It was intense. It was powerful and it seemed to consume every inch of her body. Her lips parted, opening to him. He instantly seized the opportunity and delved in. The taste of him was pure ecstasy. She moaned.

She felt his arms wrap around her, drawing her close, molding her body to his. His mouth was cemented to hers. Her body burned with hunger, want and desire. Then, he gently released her. She was breathless. It was like nothing she'd ever experienced. She leaned against him, pressing her hand to his chest to steady her mind and still her trembling legs. His heart beat wildly, matching her own.

"I'll walk you back to your room," he said.

"That's not necessary," she said. Her insides still shook with the passion he had ignited.

"I'd hate to have someone else be threatened with pepper spray."

"Humor, unexpected, not bad for a first attempt," she said.

He laughed heartedly. They took the elevator down, but instead of getting off at the lobby floor, they got off on the next floor. He guided her through the lower level and exited behind the resort right near the pool and spa. They walked first in silence then started talking about the beauty of the location and the different things to do in the area. Moments later they stopped in front of her suite. "This is me, number two," she said, biting her lower lip as she pulled her key card out of her jacket pocket. "Thank you again for the midnight snack and the conversation. I really had a great time."

"You're welcome."

"So when would these tutoring sessions begin?"

"As soon as possible. There should be no problem clearing my schedule. How about seven o'clock tomorrow?" he said.

"Okay, I'm in," she agreed, "I'll see you tomorrow evening."

"Actually, that's seven o'clock in the morning."

Shay's mouth flew open. "What? No way. That's in less than five hours from now."

"Yes, it is," he affirmed graciously.

"Well, I usually run in the mornings, but I guess I can skip it this one time."

"We'll take the lessons in progressive steps. Starting at the beginning and working our way through."

"What's the first step?" she asked, pulling her card out of the slot.

"Introduction to Romance 101," he said.

"Seven in the morning," she said, then pushed her key card into the slot and pulled it out again. The small light remained red. She tried it again. Nothing happened a second time. "So much for a graceful exit," she said.

He stepped close just behind her and took the card from her hand. He could smell the light fragrant scent of her perfume again and feel the warmth of her body pressed close to his. He pushed the key card into the slot and then eased it out slowly. The light immediately turned green and the latch released. He handed the card back to her. Their hands touched and held. "Thanks," she nearly whispered, "for everything."

"You're welcome," he said softly. "I'll see you tomorrow morning."

She nodded then they stood there lost in the moment. The coolness of the night circled them as a sudden burning heat simmered between their bodies again. The pull they felt was attraction. She looked up. He was too close or not close enough. He lowered his head, she met him halfway. They hovered a brief instant, and then their mouths connected. The kiss was slow, gentle and defining, but with underlining promises of an erupting arousal too near the surface. When it ended he backed away. "Good night," he said.

"Good night," Shay replied, and then stood in the doorway watching him walk away. "Oh, and Doc," she said softly. He stopped and turned. She shrugged. "I decided I guess you're not so bad after all."

"Who'da thunk it?" he said then winked.

She chuckled, stepped back and went inside. She leaned against the closed door and touched her lips softly, licking the barest taste of him. She could still feel the gentle pressure of his mouth. "Not bad at all," she said then went into the bathroom and turned on the cool water to take a nice refreshing shower.

Quinn walked back to the resort entrance feeling a renewed sense of motivation. His conversation with Shay told him everything he needed to know. She was perfect. He headed straight to his office, sat down at his desk, opened his computer and began writing for the first time in months. His thoughts and observations flowed like water. He saw Shay fitting into the process seamlessly. He wrote a simple question as the subtitle for his own point of reference. How to fall in love?

Shay Daniels was just what he needed. She was the perfect candidate. Her responses to him were on target and she was just skeptical enough to resist his initial advances. The challenge of seducing someone who was detached emotionally was too tempting to pass up. The question was, could he induce enough emotions to coerce the feeling of love? He outlined a seduction program just for her. The words and ideas flowed brilliantly. An hour and a half later he looked up smiling. He'd found his muse. Her name was Shay. He continued writing.

It was barely dawn when Quinn finally saved his file and closed his laptop. He'd been writing for the past three hours. His focus was unwavering and the ideas just kept coming. Shay was the perfect subject. She was cynical, detached and unimpressed. She didn't appear to have any ulterior motives and she was willing to try something new. That intrigued him—she intrigued him.

He got up, went into his bedroom, showered and climbed into bed. He smiled in the dim light. He wasn't sure what Shay had in mind, but he intended to teach her a lesson she'd never forget.

Chapter 9

The phone rang at some ungodly hour. Startled awake, Shay blindly stabbed at the alarm clock, trying to turn it off before realizing it wasn't ringing. In her frantic haste for silence, she succeeded in knocking over her cell phone, the clock radio, her bottled water and the book she fell asleep reading the night before. She finally opened her eyes and picked up the receiver. She peeked to the side of the bed and glanced at the clock on the floor. It was six o'clock in the morning. "Hello," she muttered softly, her voice still heavy and husky.

"Good morning, Ms. Daniels. Your first lesson in romance begins in one hour."

She glanced at the clock again. "One hour, you're kidding me, right? It's way too early for romance."

"It's never too early for romance. I'll see you in an hour."

"Wait," she said, sitting up too quickly, "what are we going to do today? I need to know what to wear."

"I wouldn't worry about it. Something will come to you," he assured her.

She sighed heavily, half smiling. "Okay, I'll see you in one hour." Shay hung up, closed her eyes and stretched lazily as she rolled over to look up at the ceiling. The fan above her bed turned slowly, expending as little energy as she felt she had. But still, she smiled in the muted darkness thinking about the night before. Turning and seeing Quinn standing behind her had startled her. But it wasn't because he had scared her. It was because of what she was thinking about—him. He was everything any woman could want. He was sexy and sensuous and everything about him screamed seduction. He just had to look at a woman to melt her insides.

She got up, showered and looked through her wardrobe for something appropriate to wear. She had no idea what to expect today, so she wanted to be ready for anything. "What do you wear to a lesson in romance and seduction?" she asked herself, then chose a pair of slacks and a simple knit sweater and matching cardigan. She looked at herself in the mirror. The outfit hugged her body nicely, not too tight, not too loose. She looked businesslike and professional. Approving, she styled her hair and added a touch of blush and lip gloss. "Perfect," she said, eyeing herself in the full-length mirror.

A few minutes later there was a knock on her door.

She glanced at the clock on the nightstand. He was early. She hurried and opened it, expecting to see Quinn standing there. Instead there was a bellman with an envelope and a white box with a red ribbon. He smiled happily. "Good morning. This package was delivered for you."

Shay looked at the large box puzzled. It had to be a mistake. No one knew she was staying there and she didn't order anything to be delivered. "I'm sorry, you have the wrong suite. I didn't order this."

As she attempted to close the door the bellmen spoke up quickly. "Ms. Daniels," he clarified. She stopped and nodded. "Then this is for you. It was delivered to the front desk this morning."

She smiled, opening the door wider. Jade was the only one who knew where she was staying. Thinking she must have sent her something, she accepted the envelope and package. "Thank you, hold on, I'll get you something," she said, and stepped away to get her purse.

"The tip has already been taken care of, Ms. Daniels. Have a good day." He nodded and smiled happily, then walked away.

Shay closed the door, curious about the box. She placed it on her desk and opened the envelope first. To her surprise it wasn't from Jade. It was from Quinn. It was an invitation to have breakfast with a request to feel free to wear what was in the box. She removed the lid and tissue paper finding a big beautiful scarf inside. She pulled it out. "Wow."

Large and flowing, the material was almost see-through silk chiffon and the rainbow colors were vibrant and instantly made her smile. She held it up. Curiously, it was oddly shaped, smaller on one end with exaggerated corners. It didn't matter; it was still beautiful. She wrapped the scarf around her neck, feeling the sensuous softness of the material on her body. He was certainly full of surprises. She glanced at the clock again. It was six fifty-five, time to go. She slipped on her shoes, grabbed her purse, jacket and cell phone then hurried out.

As soon as she left the suite she saw Quinn standing in the front garden waiting for her. He was leaning back perched against an iron bench talking on his cell phone. His back was turned to her, but she'd recognize him anywhere. She smiled, watching him unawares. Sexy didn't even begin to describe him. He was pure knee-weakening, mind-blowing, heart-pounding gorgeous. The light-colored brightness of his shirt was a deep contrast to his milk chocolate toned complexion. His legs were long and seemed muscular beneath his stylish dark slacks.

Her stomach fluttered as thoughts of fantasies came to mind. She knew hers, now she wondered about his. What would a single, unattached romance and relationship therapist fantasize about?

He turned as soon as she saw her. He immediately hung up as she approached. "Good morning," he said.

"Good morning. You didn't have to get off the phone for me."

"Of course I did. The first rule of romance is giving you my full, total and undivided attention. That means turning off the cell phone and everything else when I'm with you." He watched as she turned off her cell and dropped it into her purse. He nodded and openly glanced down the length of her body nodding. "You look comfortable, very professional," he said evenly.

"Thanks," she said, leaning against the back of the bench. "Okay, what's first?"

He looked down the full length of her body again. "Let's go shopping."

"Okay, for what?" she asked.

"Clothes," he said.

"Clothes. What kind of clothes do you need?"

"They won't be for me, they'll be for you."

"What's wrong with my clothes?"

"Nothing, they're fine, for work, for business, but not for what I have in mind. You need a little something extra. The first lesson, romance and seduction involve the senses, all of them. We're going to focus on some of them."

"So I presume we're doing sight first."

"Not just sight. We're also doing the visual senses of appearance, dazzle and radiance. To romance or seduce someone you need to first get their attention. The visual is the first connection. Every successful seduction begins the instant a man sees a woman or a woman sees a man. So the first glance needs to seal the deal. You must be noticed and feel worthy of being noticed. I want you to pay close attention to the change in the way men look at you throughout the day."

"Okay, sounds good," she said, "but what's open this early?"

"A friend has agreed to make her family's boutique available." She nodded. He held his hand out to her. "Let's get you started." She grasped it and leaned away from the bench. They walked back to the front of the resort. "I've made arrangements for you to move into the penthouse."

"With you?" she confirmed jokingly, as they walked into the lobby. She looked around. Surprisingly, there were quite a few people walking around.

"At times. Are you okay with that?" he asked.

"Yes," she said, looking up at the waterfall.

"Good, this way." They walked down the corridor to the small boutique beside one of the restaurants. Quinn knocked on the glass door. Alona came and opened it immediately. "Good morning," she said happily.

"Good morning," Shay said, delighted to see a smiling familiar face. She walked in and began looking around.

"Good morning, Alona," Quinn said. "Thanks again."

"No problem. I love doing this," she said excitedly.

"I'll see you later." He released the door.

Shay hurried out behind him. "Hey, wait, you're leaving?" she asked.

"Alona knows what to do. Also, you have a massage

scheduled in the penthouse at noon. We'll have lunch afterward. Enjoy your morning." A few seconds later he was gone.

Quinn headed directly to the penthouse as soon as he left Shay. He went to his desk and began working. He reviewed his writing from the night before and then formulated a working plan for the rest of the day. Shay had two and a half weeks and he intended to spend every day with her. Last night he had set everything in motion. All he had to do now was follow through. He'd teach Shay about seduction and romance and in exchange she'd teach him the emotions behind falling in love. All he had to do was observe and record. And as long as he kept his emotional distance everything would work out just as he planned.

She'd get what she wanted and he'd get what he wanted. He began writing, picking up where he left off just a few hours earlier. His breakfast was brought in, and then later removed. His water pitcher was refilled repeatedly. Time continued as he worked nearly nonstop.

After a while he glanced up at the clock. Services around the resort would be opened and he needed to make plans. He called the front desk and made arrangements to have Shay's luggage brought to the penthouse and moved into the guest room.

Then he stood and walked out onto the balcony. He looked out over the massive expanse of the Sonora Desert. The sky was crystal clear and the grounds below were tended to perfection. They were technically in the middle of barren land, but Serenity appeared as an oasis and a safe haven from the harsh reality around them.

He smiled as memories of Shay and their time together streamed through his thoughts. Just a few hours earlier they were out here kissing. He sighed heavily as his body tensed and tightened. She aroused him even in her absence. The thick, heated, uncomfortable feeling in his groin reminded him of just how long it had been. It was like he was waiting for her alone. Yes, sex was going to happen. It was a predictable and expected conclusion to his study. There was no avoidance or direction around it. He wanted it and he knew she wanted it.

Even before they'd formally met, their playful seduction in the hall pointed in that single direction. She wanted a night of passion and he was more than willing to oblige. He wondered what might have happened if they'd met later in the evening. A satisfied smile tipped his lips. She was certainly the one.

Theoretically he had factored sex into his equation, but for some reason it seemed different now. He didn't know if it was the fact that he was getting so close to the end result or the fact that it would be with Shay. Either way, he anticipated the moment with ardent excitement and an intense arousal.

He went back to his office and picked up his cell and called Danny to find out if he had any more information.

"I don't have much more than I gave you last night.

She's pretty far under the radar. Have you decided on her?"

"Yes. I think she'll be fine."

"You've only got two weeks. That's not a lot of time to examine the feeling of falling in love. What if it doesn't happen?"

"It will."

"Are you sure?"

"It will," he repeated. "Anything else going on?"

"*The Sensual Seduction* has gone into another printing. I'm not sure which number this is now, but your publisher wants to send a private jet to fly you in and celebrate. They also want to talk to you about signing another contract. Since you passed on their last offer, they're hustling to come up with something new."

"They're gonna have to offer me the world to even consider signing again."

"I would be surprised if they didn't. They know your popularity and they're trying to tie you down before you jump ship."

"I'm going to be busy the next few days."

"They're also willing to come see you."

"Busy."

Danny chuckled. "No problem, I'll pass it on. Also, Nola called last night. She got a call from a friend of hers in L.A. They want to do a movie based on you and your books. There's already a treatment planned."

Quinn laughed. "No, definitely not."

Danny chuckled. "Yep, I already turned it down."

"I'm headed back to my place. I'll talk to you later."

* * *

Shay had gone back inside the boutique after her quick conversation with Quinn. Alona smiled welcomingly. "We've got some great new merchandise in. I've already pulled some aside. Some of the clothes are going to look spectacular on you." She looked at her watch. "Okay, we've got breakfast foods, tea, orange juice and three hours until the store opens. We'd better get started."

Shay followed Alona as she began showing her all the clothes she pulled out earlier. Shay selected a dozen pieces to try on. She went into the dressing room and got busy. Thirty minutes later the room looked as if it had been hit by a cyclone. There were dresses, skirts, blouses, pants, even bras and panties hanging all over the room. "What about lingerie?" Shay asked after trying on the fifth or sixth outfit.

"If the clothes you just picked out look as fabulous as I think they will, believe me, you won't need any lingerie, at least not for long."

Shay smiled and winked. "Good point. So, your family owns the boutique."

"Yes, we have a silent partner, but he's always extremely silent."

Shay understood that Quinn was the partner without Alona needing to elaborate. "You have so many beautiful things here."

"We're getting ready for the Sonora Equinox Party."

"What's the Sonora Equinox Party?"

"The resort sponsors the party every year. It celebrates

the beginning of spring and also raises money for the foundation. It's all night long from the official time to sunrise. This year it's on the twentieth and starts at twenty-three:twenty-one. It ends on the twenty-first at sunrise. It's always packed. All the restaurants and shops are open and people come from all over to enjoy it. There will be music, auctions and headliner singers and bands, dancing and celebrities and all kinds of food."

"Wow, it sounds like fun. I can't wait. I've never heard about it before."

"Dr. Anderson started it right after he bought Serenity. That was four years ago. It's been getting bigger and bigger ever since."

"Question. How well do you know Quinn?"

"Some, he's my boss."

"What's he like?"

"He's a good guy, he's caring and generous. He's really focused on his work. He doesn't laugh much 'cause he's very serious. He's honest and cool. And he's really good at what he does. I just got married because of him."

"Congratulations."

"Thanks. I don't know, some people say he's incapable of settling down again after his wife died five years ago. I don't think so. I think he just needs the right woman, someone who challenges him."

"Doesn't he date a lot?"

"Not really. He's always busy working. But when he does, it never seems to work out. Like everybody, he's looking for that special someone," she said, and then picked up another blouse, "I love this. It just came in. What do you think?"

"It's gorgeous."

"Wait, I forgot, I have the perfect dress." Alona grabbed it and held it up. "It's the only one that came in and it looks like it's your size."

Shay looked at the midnight-blue halter dress and nodded her head slowly. "Oh, man, that is too sexy. It will definitely get a man's attention and keep it." Alona nodded, agreeing. Shay took the dress and tried it on. It fit perfectly, every curve, every line molded to her body faultlessly.

Alona came to the dressing room. "Oh, you look sensational. Wait, I think I have just the shoes for you." She hurried out then came back a few minutes later with a pair of strappy stilettos. Shay tried them on, noticed they fitted great, then turned and looked at herself in the mirror. Alona nodded. "You're gonna knock someone's socks off in that outfit."

"Good, that's the whole idea."

Alona headed back to the front of the store. Shay changed, taking special care with the stunning blue dress. She continued trying on clothes for another hour. When she finally picked out everything she wanted she changed back into her original outfit. Alona was waiting for her in the front of the store. "Here's your key card to the penthouse suite. Your luggage is already there. I'll have everything here delivered within the hour."

"Thank you," Shay said.

"One more thing. I found a few other accessories

you might need," Alona said. She held up a hanger and smiled.

Shay nodded her complete agreement. "Oh yes, absolutely."

Fifteen minutes later the store opened. Shay finished in plenty of time. She had chosen seven complete new outfits and a few little special somethings. "Thank you for all your help, Alona. You've been wonderful."

"You're very welcome. Everything has been charged to your room and will be delivered within the hour."

"Excellent."

"Is there anything else I can help you with?"

"No, you were wonderful. Thank you."

"You're very welcome. I enjoy being a personal shopper. Everything will be sent to the penthouse."

Shay left the store and headed directly to the elevator Quinn took her to the night before. She looked at her watch. It was ten-fifteen and she still had some time before her massage. She wanted to go up to the penthouse and have a quick talk with Quinn.

Using her key card, she went in and called out his name. He wasn't there. She looked around in his office area, the kitchen and then opened the glass doors and went out onto the balcony. In the light of day the terrace was much longer and larger than she remembered. There was even a small Jacuzzi on the side.

She walked over to the railing and looked out at the view. It was just as she remembered, only better. She began thinking about the past few years. The travel was wearing her down. She was on the road at least nine months out of the year. No wonder she couldn't sustain a lasting relationship. No wonder she kept getting dumped. But she loved her job and wasn't ready to stop.

Realizing it was just before eleven, she went back in, locked the balcony doors and went upstairs to her suite to get ready for her massage. There were three suites. She chose the first, went inside and looked around. She immediately saw this was hers. As promised, her luggage had not only been delivered to the penthouse suite, but all her clothes had been put away. Her phone charger had been plugged in again and the book she'd been reading was on the nightstand, just as it had been in the other suite.

She picked it up and lay back on the comfortable lounge chair to read. Soon she was completely engrossed. Before, she'd only flipped through his book, snatching quick sentences here and there. This time she read more thoroughly. Jade was right. It was good. Dr. Love was insightful and articulate. She glanced across the room at the clock. It had gotten late. She hurriedly undressed and grabbed a quick shower. When she got out she dried off then slipped on a pair of panties and put on one of the guest robes she found in the bathroom. She went back into the bedroom and decided to relax for a few minutes and continue reading. She picked up a book and lay down on the chaise again. That's when she heard it.

There was soft music playing downstairs. She went to the second-floor balcony overlooking the den. No one was there, but the balcony doors were open again. She went downstairs. There was a man standing with his back to her looking out at the view. She looked around, seeing that a massage table had been set up while she was in the shower. He was obviously her masseur. She took a moment to admire his body. He was dressed casually in jeans and a simple white T-shirt. She boldly looked up and down the length of his body, admiring every visible inch.

His shoulders were wide, his back was broad and his waist was oh-so-nicely narrow. His arms were muscled, but not exaggerated like some men. He worked out but didn't seem to make it a religion. And most important, he definitely looked like he knew what he was doing. She smiled as arousing thoughts streamed through her mind. Her lying on the table and him freely touching every inch of her. How interesting would that be. She bit her lower lip as she admired his tight rounded rear and then his long slightly bowed legs. She briefly considered that he was part of her seduction lesson. Then reality intruded and she took a deep breath and allowed the thoughts to fade.

She stepped outside. "Hi, I guess you're my masseur," she said, getting his attention. He turned around. Her jaw dropped. "Quinn, I thought we were having lunch *after* my massage."

"We are. I'll be massaging you this afternoon."

"You?" she said then repeated, "You?" She tried unsuccessfully to get the idea through her head. He had to be joking. This was asking way too much. After the kiss last night she wasn't sure how much more she could take. Maybe this wasn't such a good idea. It had been almost nine months since a man had intimately touched her. Bruce wasn't exactly an expert or even remotely talented in that area. That meant she was already set to explode. The kiss had already lit the fuse, now having Quinn touch her was going to ignite the fire.

"Yes, your next lesson is learning how to relax during the seduction." He walked over to the massage table already set up by the pool. "Are you ready for me?" he asked, with the sexiest half smile she'd ever seen. He picked up a large white sheet. She nodded slowly, knowing this was insane. "Good, come on over." She took a deep breath and began walking over to him. With each step she felt more goose pimples on her skin and her heart pounded so loudly that she was sure he could hear it. "Turn around," he said softly. She turned. He draped the sheet over his arm and then reached around her waist and loosened the robe's ties. Her nerve endings went into overdrive.

"Seduction is all about stimulating the senses. It's a mind-set and you need to be completely relaxed to enjoy it. You worked on enhancing your outward appearance this morning. When a man sees you in a crowded room, you must be the only woman he sees. What you wear is key, but how you wear it is essential. This afternoon we'll explore relaxation methods and the sense of touch and feel." Shay closed her eyes. He eased the robe slowly off her shoulders.

She stood topless facing away from him. He placed his large hands on her shoulders and gently kneaded her tight muscles. She immediately released. He rubbed his thumbs down the center length of her neck several times. She could feel her body sway with the slow, sensuous rhythm of his touch. "Are you ready for me?" he asked again. She nodded. He tossed the robe and wrapped the white sheet around her body. She secured it in front then turned around to him. Standing here with him this close, she could sense every nerve in her body tingling. Her heart raced and her breathing was quick and shallow.

"Step up and have a seat."

She looked down, noticing for the first time that a step stool had been placed beside the table. She gathered the sheet around her, stepped up and sat down on the table. He tucked the steps beneath the table and picked up a warmed bottle and poured a heated liquid into his hands. She watched as he rubbed them together then moved closer, taking her hands in his. "For this to work you're going to have trust me, let go and relax," he said as he rubbed his hands gently. "Can you do that?"

She nodded her head then whispered, "Yes."

"Good, close your eyes. Trust, relax and enjoy."

She closed her eyes again. Her heart pounded in her chest and her thoughts swam dizzily and he was only holding her hands. What was she going to do when he actually began touching her? He released her hands and touched the sheet. Her eyes popped open. He was smiling at her as he grabbed the top hem securely. "Lay back," he instructed, releasing and holding the sheet up as she did. A scintillating sense of anticipation swept over her.

He guided the large sheet comfortably loose across her body. She lay down and he began, as promised, to stimulate her senses. He gently smoothed her arm at her side and then pressed his hands down the length of her body. Down her thigh to her leg then to her feet then back up on the other side. He smoothed and pressed her other arm, then worked his way across her shoulders. Then he stopped. She opened her eyes and saw him pick up the bottle again and rub his hands together. She had no idea where he'd start first.

He turned. Their eyes connected. She wasn't sure what she saw in his, but she knew that if he was half as astute as she thought he was, he knew exactly what she was feeling. She closed her eyes. Then she felt him. He was standing at the head of the table. He placed his hands on her shoulders, holding her still a few moments. Then he applied a little pressure and she felt her body release and let go.

She heard him walk the length of the table then stop at the far end. He touched her feet and began massaging the soles and her toes. Taking each one, he slowly and methodically worked each, applying just enough pressure to send chills through her body. Then he released her feet and concentrated on her legs. His hands were masterful. He rubbed and caressed her calves, her legs and her thighs. She released the tension she'd been holding as her body had begun to give way and enjoy the feeling. Then he took her hand, separating each finger and tenderly rubbing to release all tension. He massaged her arms and then leaned close. "Roll over."

He held the sheet as she rolled to her stomach. She lay facedown tucking her face into the cushioned well. He readjusted the sheet to just below her back. Then, as soon as he touched again, there was an electric connection. She had long since relaxed, but now she drifted to another place altogether. She wasn't asleep, she was just completely tranquil. Suddenly every subtle nuance of the moment was enhanced. She heard music, but not just the soft jazz playing in the room. She also heard birds and water flowing in the distance. She heard a jet flying miles overhead. She smelled the lavender oil on her body and his delicately spicy cologne. There was also the lingering scent and last remnants of the shower gel she used earlier. Everything seemed clearer or maybe it was just her. Either way, she was loving it.

Chapter 10

Her mind wandered and fantasy images appeared in a haze of semiconsciousness. Everything around her seemed to change. What was once midday was now night. The room was dark, illuminated only by a few candles and the fireplace in the corner. They were out in the middle of the desert, but somehow still on the balcony. There were a million stars above them. The air was cool, but she didn't feel it. All she could feel was Quinn. The sheet was gone, she lay completely naked. He stood at the head of the table again. He continued massaging her, but now it was more passionate and more intense. She lay on her back as his hands moved across her silky skin, first to her neck, then her shoulders then her chest and finally her breasts. She breathed deeply, luxuriating in the feel of his powerful hands.

She watched the thick braided muscles in his arms as they tensed and flexed in easy movement. He dipped down to her breasts again, cupping them. He kneaded them tenderly, allowing his thumbs to taunt and tease her already pebbled nipples. She arched her body up. His mouth came down to her neck, kissing and licking her. She moaned. Her mouth opened. He was there instantly, inside. His tongue delved deep. His hands continued their ravishing ways. Then all of a sudden he was beside the table feasting on her body. He captured her breast, pulling, suckling and licking the already hard nipple. Her body writhed with need and want as he tickled her with his tongue. She surged with desire.

She rolled over and suddenly he was behind her. She was on her knees and felt the stone hardness of his penis as he wrapped his hands around her body. She gasped as his hand came down between her legs and captured her treasure. He was gentle and protective. His fingers slid inside as the palm of his other hand continued circling the tip of her nipple. Her legs trembled. Her body weakened. Their bodies molded together as she rocked her hips up and down. They easily fell into a rhythm. Every nerve in her body sizzled.

Then he released her, grabbed her waist and hips and easily turned her to face him. She looked up into his eyes. They were dark, dilated and intense. She straddled his hips, wrapping her legs around him tightly. He held then picked her up. In one smooth motion he pulled her close, impaling her onto the throbbing hardness of his penis. She gasped and shrieked her abrupt pleasure. The tightness instantly gave way to the feel of him inside of her. Then slowly the feeling faded as the brightness of day returned.

Her eyes fluttered open slowly. She was lying on her stomach and it was daytime again. She realized she'd been dreaming, fantasizing. But it was so real, a part of her wasn't sure if it really happened or not. Quinn's hands continued to soothe her body as he centered on her back, neck and shoulders again. He grabbed her waist and held tight, then released her and leaned in. "How do you feel?" he whispered.

"I feel—" she began, then inhaled deeply and released what could be considered a near purr as she exhaled "—amazing."

"Excellent. That means you're done," he said. She immediately rolled over and tried to get up. "No, no, relax a minute, get your bearings," he said. "Take your time getting up, you might feel a little light-headed or dizzy."

Shay nodded and lay back down, closing her eyes again. He was so right, she was so done. Her body was so relaxed she could barely move, let alone get up and walk. His hands were magical. Every muscle in her body seemed to just melt. She eased back and let the last few moments sink in. Here she was, lying in a near stranger's penthouse with nothing on but a thin sheet draped across her body and she was completely calm and tranquil. She would have never thought that possible.

She shook her head in amazement. He was having an interesting effect on her already. "That was fantastic," she said dreamily.

He leaned over to say something, but stopped. Instead he looked at the sweet perfection of her face. She was so lovely. The perfect symmetry and her features were unmistakable. Her eyes were closed and she was half smiling as if she'd just been told a private joke and was savoring the punch line. He wanted to touch her again, but he knew he couldn't. The massage had already set his body on fire. Lava burned in his blood and rampaged through his veins. He reminded himself it wasn't about him, it was about the project. He took a deep breath and released it slowly. "Seduction is often about the chase, not necessary about the conquest. So it will be up to you to entice the chase, to keep it going. Make it interesting. Surprise him. Remember, to seduce, always stimulate the senses."

She opened her eyes and saw him just inches from her mouth. She didn't respond and he didn't say anything else. They just stared at each other. She waited for him to kiss her, but he didn't. He leaned away and held her robe open. She sat up slowly, turned and slipped it on, allowing the sheet to drop to the tile floor. She wrapped the front without tying the sash then wobbled slightly. He held her shoulders steady, bringing her intimately close to his body. She immediately felt the firmness of his arousal against her back.

"Steady," he said crisply.

She nodded and turned. "Thank you, for everything."

He nodded, released her and then stepped back and leaned against the table. "I'll be right down," she said, walking back into the penthouse, then she stopped and returned back to him. "Quinn," she said, seeing him in the same position only with his head lowered. He looked up. "These lessons, I'm curious, am I supposed to be seducing you or are you supposed to be seducing me?"

"That is always up to you. Time to get dressed. Our lunch reservation is in one hour."

He didn't answer her question. She was getting used to that. "Are we going out?" she asked.

He nodded. "We're going to the Serenity Garden Restaurant downstairs. It's one of the many award-winning restaurants in the area. The setting is as exciting as the menu."

"I remember seeing it earlier. It looks amazing from the outside."

"It is. I think you'll enjoy it."

Her eyes shone even though she didn't quite feel joyful inside. "Sounds great," she said with ease. "I won't be long." She turned and went back into the penthouse to go up to her bedroom suite.

Quinn watched her turn and walk away a second time. Before moving, he took a moment to get himself together. Just that quickly she had gotten to him. He took a deep breath and released it gradually as he continued leaning back against the side of the table. He shook his head slowly then looked down at his hands. They didn't shake or tremble, they didn't look any different, but the silky softness of her body was still making them tingle. He wanted her. He tightened his hands into fists in hopes of controlling his hunger. She was too tempting and his body was too needful.

Thankfully he had regained control of his wayward body. But there was certainly a feeling he hadn't felt or expected to feel in a long time. In the years since his wife died, he had trained himself to be detached and impassive. He had chosen to remove himself from all emotional connections. He couldn't afford the luxury of sentiment, particularly when it came to his work. Now, for him it was always all about the science. Things, people, women, seldom affected him. He didn't allow it. Now he couldn't stop it even if he wanted to.

Admittedly, some had come close. Others had tried every trick and maneuver in their arsenal to get to him or win his affection. Even when he allowed himself pleasure, it was always on his terms. He made sure they knew up front that he wouldn't get emotionally involved. Some didn't believe. Others chose to openly challenge him thinking he'd bend. He never did. None of them succeeded. He was always in control. But what he was feeling now was different. His control had slipped the second he laid eyes on her and it had been steadily falling ever since.

Holding her was more for his benefit than for hers and he knew it. The subtle curve of her body as she gathered the silk robe around her tested his resolve and made his body shudder and tense. When he looked down he had easily distinguished her heart-shaped rear as the sweet sway of her hips set in action. He remembered how close he came to stripping the sheet away and joining her on the table. She'd moved quickly, but for him it seemed to take a lifetime.

The needful yearn in his loins returned. But he couldn't go there now. He turned away quickly. He couldn't continue watching her. His pants tightened across the front and his body began yearning as thoughts of his hands touching her began to test his determination. He had to remain focused. He couldn't yield to his body's needs. He picked up and twisted the lid tightly on the bottle of oil he'd used for the massage. He held it a second then twisted it even tighter.

Moments later he went into the office and sat down at his desk. He opened his laptop and started typing, then stopped a few minutes later. He glanced up toward the second floor, hearing the soft hum of the shower. A slow lustful smile tipped his full lips. Imagining her naked and wet sent his body into overdrive. He thought about their kiss the night before. It was passionate and promising and kept him up far later than he'd expected. Now, knowing that she'd be just down the hall from him was tempting his control again. He felt the tightness in his pants and the blazing heat simmer through his body. She was getting to him. He closed the laptop and decided to grab a quick cold shower before lunch. As soon as he stood, the office phone rang. He walked back to the desk and grabbed it quickly. "Yeah."

"Good, you're still there. It's Danny. I have great news

for you. *Psychology Today* found out about your study with the university and they want *you* for next issue's cover story."

"Wow, that's fantastic."

"Yeah, they want to do a whole issue centered on your study and the process of falling in love. They're talking about lining up major sponsors and doing a full media campaign including reviewing and promoting your book when it's released."

"That's great. Does the university know?"

"Not yet, I just found out and called you first. This is going to be major funding for the school."

Quinn smiled excitedly. This was the news he'd been waiting to hear. This study would definitely change the direction of his work and his career. "What's the new time frame?"

"Everything has to be accelerated," Danny said. "The magazine wants a few quotes and an excerpt as soon as possible. So the time frame is going to have to be moved up. The four weeks is now two weeks at most. Is that going to be a problem?"

Quinn looked up at the second level. Shay was key to his study. Everything he had done, all the research and studies now depended on her. And keeping her in the dark was essential. "It shouldn't be. I'll let you know."

"One more thing. Your publisher called. As requested, they just offered you the world," Danny said. Quinn laughed. Danny joined in. "I'll call you tomorrow."

Quinn hung up then went upstairs with a renewed spirit of accomplishment and anticipation. His end goal was close and now he needed to fast forward his research. He went to the master bedroom, quickly undressed and set the showerhead's jets to full blast then stepped beneath the onslaught. The punishing blast was just what he expected: fierce. But he needed it. He needed to get back to his focus. The case study was the important thing, not his physical discomfort. He needed to step back and regroup and take it up a notch.

Seeing her and touching her had affected him more than he imagined it would. His body was already on a low simmer ever since the public seduction. Then the temperature rose through the roof after their kiss the night before. But he needed the research and had to be personally involved. He was the only one who could do it because firsthand knowledge was essential for this study.

After the shower he dressed in casual pants and a shirt then went downstairs. Since Shay was still in her bedroom, he went back into the office, opened his laptop and began typing.

As soon as Shay closed the bedroom door behind her she dropped the robe and went directly into the shower. When she got out she realized the clothes she'd bought earlier that day had not only been delivered, but like her other clothes, had been hung up and put away. She chose her favorite pair of slacks and a summer knit top with matching cardigan. She put them on then looked at herself in the mirror. She looked professional. Then she realized she was doing exactly what she always did.

She was playing it safe. She went back into the closet, hung the cardigan up and pulled out one of the new tops she'd got. It was a low wrapped V-neck sleeveless silk blouse with a loose ruffle in front set on a diagonal to accent her breasts. She tried it on then looked at herself in the mirror. She arched forward and stood more erect. It didn't work. She removed her bra and tried it again. It fit her perfectly and it seemed to change her whole attitude.

Smiling her approval, she finished dressing, styled her hair and was just about to leave the room when her cell phone rang. She answered quickly, knowing she still had a few extra minutes before lunch. "Hello."

"Hey, how's it going? Any luck with the interview?" Jade asked.

"Would you believe I'm standing in Quinn Anderson's penthouse suite at Serenity right now?"

"Very funny," Jade said sarcastically.

"I'm serious. We met last night at the forum then again after his conference. We started talking then one thing led to another. He volunteered to help me get my romance center back."

"Wait, you're serious."

"Yeah, I am."

"OMG, was that you on the video from the forum? I saw it this morning. It's from somebody's cell phone. It shows Dr. Love talking to some woman, but you can barely see her face."

"I don't know, sounds like it."

"Do you have any idea how incredible this is? You

have to tell me everything and don't you dare leave anything out."

"Actually I can't right now. I'm on my way out. But I'll call you later and we'll talk."

"You'd better."

Shay half smiled as she stepped out of her room and looked down the short hallway to the other bedrooms. She knew one of them was his. She didn't know which. Then, hearing talking she glanced down at the conversation pit area of the penthouse. "I gotta go. We're headed to lunch in a few."

"Okay, don't forget to call me."

"I'll catch up with you later." As soon as she came downstairs she heard the sound of typing. She followed the sound to the office doorway just beyond the conference room area. Quinn was at his desk on the laptop. She presumed he was working on his next book. She stood in the doorway watching him. He didn't look up at first, but stayed focused on his work. Then he glanced up, sensing her.

He sat back, smiling. "You look delicious."

"Thanks, that's exactly what I was going for. May I?"

"Sure, come on in."

"Working on your next book?"

"Actually it's a study I've been working on. Chances are it will turn into a book later." He pressed a few keys then removed his flash drive.

"What's it about, seduction, fantasies or love?"

"All of the above, but mostly love. Are you ready to

go?" he asked. She nodded happily. He stood up and walked to her, looking into her deep sultry eyes as she approached. "Let's go." They got in the elevator and went down to the lobby. She turned toward the Serenity Garden Restaurant they spoke about earlier, but he took her arm and guided her to the exit instead.

"I thought we were going here," she said.

"Actually, I have a better idea," he said. They quickly passed through the lobby and ended up outside. She looked both ways, wondering what his better idea might be. "This way," he said, guiding her to a small silver sports car parked a few feet from the entrance.

"Yours?" she asked. He nodded. She shook her head. "I would have expected something more sedate. So where are we headed?"

"I thought you might like to see the city up close and personal."

She nodded. "That sounds perfect."

Chapter 11

The sporty convertible was fast and fun and Quinn drove like a seasoned professional. Each curve and bend was maneuvered precisely, perfectly. Music played and the powerful engine roared, making the enjoyable ride even more exciting. For the first ten minutes neither spoke, each enjoyed the exhilarating ride. Shay looked around at the picturesque beauty they passed. Ideally this was exactly what she needed, peace away from the city and away from the cable show. This was the perfect escape. She had been pent-up and stressed out for too long. But peace and serenity wasn't all she needed anymore. She inhaled deeply, smelling the delicate scent of Quinn's cologne. She knew exactly what she needed.

She looked over at Quinn. He turned to her that exact same instant. Their eyes met. A flash of heat shot through her, setting her body on fire. She smiled slightly and quickly looked away, trying to concentrate on the scenery again, but it was impossible. All she could think about now was Quinn. She closed her eyes and rested her head back. Not even the balmy breeze and warm sun on her face eased her wants this time.

"Am I going too fast for you, making you nervous?" Quinn asked, after having glanced over and seen her eyes closed.

She opened her eyes and looked at him quickly then faced forward. "No, not at all. I was just thinking how incredible this is, being here. It's not exactly something I get to do a lot in the city."

"Perhaps you should consider moving."

"What, and give up the Big Apple, never," she declared righteously.

"Why not? I did," he said, slowing the car down making their conversation easier to be heard.

She looked over at him again. "Wait, I thought this was your hometown?"

"It is, now. But I was born and raised in Manhattan."

She started laughing. "Manhattan, you?"

"Is that hard to believe?" he asked.

"Yes, totally," she said. "So, how did you come to live here in Arizona of all places?"

"I went to the University of Arizona after high school and realized the world was a lot bigger than I thought. I stayed here until I finished."

"So you came here and never went back."

"No, I go back all the time. But this is my home now. There's sunshine three hundred and fifty days a year, the crime rate is low, the housing market is thriving, we have everything you can possibly imagine—spas, shopping, rodeos, art galleries, museums, hiking, horseback riding, historic culture, you name it. It's a one-of-a-kind experience living here," he said, then looked over at her. She was smiling. "I guess I sound like a travel brochure."

"No, not at all. You sound like you've made a wonderful home for yourself. What more can anyone want?"

He glanced over at her again. "There's always more."

She turned to him. Their eyes locked for a few seconds. She saw something then he turned back. Moments later traffic slowed and congested as they neared the city. Quinn continued to loosen up even more talking about his favorite places to travel. He was charming and fascinating. He talked about the versatile history of Arizona starting with the Hohokam Indians, then the Spanish and then the freed slaves and the European influence. He pointed out numerous places of interest and talked about their history.

After a while the conversation lapsed into a comfortable silence. Still they seemed to sync perfectly as each sat back and enjoyed the slow, steady flow lost in their own thoughts. Shay looked out the open window admiring the vast horizon around her. Everything seemed flat and two-dimensional compared to New York's massive vertical structures. "What's that over there, a school?" she asked, pointing to a mass of large structures in the distance.

"That's one of the University of Arizona campuses, my alma mater. I went there for my undergrad, grad and finally my PhD studies. Now I'm a visiting scholar. I guest lecture a class a few times a semester. I have an important study to present there in a couple of weeks."

"So, what do you teach?"

"What else, the psychology of love."

"Now how exactly does one teach the psychology of love? Isn't love pretty much abstract in practice and theory? How can you actually teach something like that?"

"The idea of love can be broken down into several distinct classifications, a few of them being agape, Eros, ludus, manic, pragma, storage or Philos and theia mania."

"What does all that mean?"

"Agape is nonsexual and selfless love, more on the line of Godly or brotherly love. Eros, named from the Greek mythology, is passionate, romantic and sexual love. Ludus is love by conquest similar to amount over substance. Manic love is obsessive and often unrequited. Pragma is rational love based on reason. Storge or Philos is kindred love through friendship."

"And the last one, theia mania, what's that?"

"It's Greek for the 'madness from the gods' or

more commonly, love at first sight. It's not specifically qualified by science. With that there's an instant attraction that is without reason or explanation. It's overwhelming and consuming. It's by mythology understanding a phenomenon unmatched by any."

"That must be hard on psychologists. How do you explain something so unexplainable?"

"At first sight is usually a margin of about point-twelve seconds. That's how long it takes for the average person to take a glimpse of someone. That, of course, is based on a person's outward appearance. The next few seconds is a predetermined subconscious take on compatibility. But the bottom line in all this is that love can only truly be defined by the person experiencing it."

"That's a lot of love."

"Actually, it's not nearly enough," he said, glancing over briefly. She was turned away in profile. The smile on her face was subtle and still beautiful.

As they neared the city the traffic began to thin out. Soon he was able to drive through the streets with relative ease. He pointed out the old Pima County Courthouse and St. Augustine Cathedral as he passed. In the arts district they turned down a small side lane then he parked the car. He got out and walked around to the passenger side to open the door. He held his hand to help her out. She grasped it and eased out. They stood chest to chest. She looked up into his eyes. They were soulful and penetrating. She pressed even closer as her stomach fluttered, her heart thundered and every nerve in her body seemed to stand on end. Her hands trembled as she touched his arms to steady herself.

The opportunity presented itself. This time she wasn't going to wait for him. Without hesitation she leaned in and kissed him. Their lips met gingerly at first, and then seconds later the full force of the moment awakened their hunger. She opened to him and he delved penetrating deep. Their tongues danced in an explosion of passion, thrusting in and out over and over again. The force of the kiss staggered her. He wrapped his strong arms around her body and pulled her closer, nearly sweeping her off her feet. She molded then melted against him. It had been too long and she was too ready. She felt the stiff hardness of his body, the firm pulse of his near erection. She was losing control. They both were.

When the embrace ended she leaned back breathless and looked into his needful eyes. It seemed they reached the same conclusion at the same time. It was the wrong place and the wrong time. He kissed her again. This time it was slow and promising, ending with delicate nibbles to her neck and shoulder. "Wrong place," he whispered.

She nodded slowly. "Wrong time."

"What is it about you that makes me…" he began, then paused.

"Makes you what?" she asked.

"Makes me want you so much," he confessed. She didn't answer. He reached up and gently stroked the side of her face, tracing down her jaw to her neck and across her shoulder. "What happened yesterday started something. Then we kissed. You feel it, don't you?" She nodded, agreeing with him. "And right now I want you so badly."

The stark seriousness of his expression stoked the already burning fire she was feeling. Her heart beat wildly and a hot flush swept over her instantly. She wanted him, too. "What do you suggest we do about it?" she asked. Her voice was deeper and huskier than usual.

"See where this leads us."

That was exactly what she wanted to hear. She stepped closer, extinguishing the scant space between their bodies. They were chest to chest again as she looked up into his needful eyes. "Right now," she said breathlessly.

He looked around. There were people everywhere, walking down the street, in stores, standing on the corners, driving by in cars. Thankfully no one paid them much attention. "Later," he promised.

"What about your research on seduction. Wouldn't we compromise your research?"

"Not at all," he said, leaning close to her ear. "If anything it will enhance it. Sexuality and the sexual experience is part of the seduction process."

Shay's body shivered despite the ninety-degree temperature. "So what do you suggest we do now?"

"Eat lunch."

She nodded, smiling. "Okay, sounds reasonable."

He nodded. "Let's go," he said, stepping back and taking her hand. She nodded, hoping her legs still worked. They did, barely. Hand in hand they strolled the short half block distance to the restaurant. As soon as they entered the maître d' walked over to welcome Quinn personally. He extended warm greetings as he led them to a secluded table in the rear of the restaurant. They sat and the maître d' told them about the day's specials. When he left they looked at each other wantonly.

"Looking at me like that is making this hard."

"You have no idea," he quipped, with a sexy half smile.

She smiled, understanding his not-so-subtle innuendo. The waiter arrived and took their drink order. As soon as he left Shay arched her fingers and leaned on the table. "Okay, change of subject. Tell me about your family. Do you have brothers and sisters?" she asked, hoping neutral conversation would cool the burning need in her body. It didn't so far. Thankfully the drinks arrived. As soon as the waiter placed her drink in front of her she picked it up and took a long sip. The refreshing iced tea chilled her throat instantly. They looked at the menu then placed their meal order. She ordered the tilapia special and he ordered grilled salmon. When the waiter left again, he answered her question. "I'm an only child. My parents divorced shortly after I was born."

"Divorced, wow, I didn't expect to hear that," she said, looking at him puzzled. "That's strange, isn't it?"

"Actually it's not so unusual. The average divorce rate in the United States fluctuates around forty-nine percent, give or take a few points."

"But you're a therapist. Not only that, you specialize in romance, relationships and love. I would have thought your parents were still together and still crazy about each other."

He laughed openly. "No, definitely not. My parents can barely stand to be in the same state, let alone the same room. I have one picture of them together."

"Really?" she asked. He nodded. "How is that possible? You're Dr. Love. You can do anything."

"You seem to have this very inflated image of me. That's not who I am."

"That's not what I keep hearing," she said.

"From whom?" he asked.

She looked at him, cocking her head to the side in astonishment. "Are you kidding? Obviously you didn't see that outrageously long line of fans waiting for you after the forum. People live their lives by your books. You change lives just by typing a sentence."

"My books aren't supposed to change lives. They're supposed to make people think and understand the process of forming healthy working relationships."

"Fine, so why not fix your parents?"

"I don't fix people and I don't work miracles."

"You know what I mean."

"The couples and people I counsel come to me with specific needs. If I can help them, I do. But they come wanting to be helped. Believe me, my parents are quite happy in their mutual hostilities."

"So, do you date a lot?" she asked him.

"No, not often, I work a lot. I haven't had a serious

relationship in a very long time. What about you?" he asked.

She shook her head no. "I'm usually too busy or away on assignment. It's kind of hard to sustain a meaningful relationship when you're always flying off to some romantic location with a film crew in tow."

"Tell me more about your job. It sounds very fulfilling."

"I wouldn't exactly say that now. But it used to be. I used to enjoy talking to honeymooners and people in love about what brought them together and what they hoped for their futures. Seeing and hearing their joy was encouraging. But one of my responsibilities is also keeping in touch with some of the couples I've interviewed over the years. Unfortunately, the majority of them are divorced, separated or broken up. It kind of deflates the happily ever after idea."

"Ahh, I see it affected you."

"I didn't think so at first, but after a while I guess it did."

Their food arrived. Everything looked delicious. They began eating as their conversation continued. "Tell me about your family. Where did you grow up?" he asked.

"I'm an only child, too. I grew up in New York. We had a small apartment. My mom is my biggest cheerleader. She's fun and funny with a lot of friends. She was a high school teacher then quit to become a paralegal."

"Why not an attorney?" he asked.

"The idea of billable hours was too confining for her. As a paralegal she can control her workload. She's always been very independent. My father was a long-distance trucker. I remember he was away most of the time. But when he was there, it was great. He'd take me to the ice cream parlor down the street and tell me all about his road trips. I used to think his truck could fly. I had a map of the United States that I made for some class project. My mom helped me so it was nearly perfect. I worked so hard on it because I wanted to keep it and see all the places he went. He'd call from the road and tell me where he was and I'd find it on my map. I'd try to plot how long it would take for him to get back home. I never quite got that part right."

"Is he a trucker still?" he asked.

"No, he retired then he was killed in a car accident a week later. Someone ran a red light and slammed into his car. He was killed instantly. He left one morning and that afternoon he was gone. It never seemed real to me. I always expected him to walk through the front door and we'd go for ice cream and talk about all the places he'd been."

"I'm sorry," Quinn said softly as he held her hand.

"My mother was devastated. They loved each other so much. They had so many plans to be together. To this day she's never gotten over it. I don't think she ever will. She still loves him. There's no room in her heart for anyone else." She paused and took a breath. Saying the words always troubled her heart. She looked at Quinn, sensing he was the same. His wife died suddenly and he'd probably never get over her, either. "She's so alone and she's such a wonderful woman."

"Hearts heal in their own time. Give her time. She'll find her way back to love again. She has you and that's her start."

Lunch ended an hour later. Instead of going back to the car they walked for a while. They looked in windows and even stopped in a few small boutiques. Quinn was stopped several times on the street and asked for his autograph or a photo. He obliged happily as Shay stepped to the side waiting. At one point she quickly stepped into a boutique, having seen something she liked in the window. By the time she purchased the item and came outside Quinn was ready and waiting.

"Are you ready to head back?"

"Sure." They turned back to the car. "So, tell me, do you like the fame part of all this?" she asked.

"It's part of the job. I enjoy the job."

"You do that a lot."

"Do what?"

"Not really answer questions. I guess it's a shrink thing."

He chuckled and gathered her into his arms and kissed her neck. Her wit was spontaneous and joyful. Her humor was infectious and being with her was getting to be addictive. It had been a long time since he'd just let himself go and enjoy the moment. He lectured it and he talked it, but seldom allowed himself the luxury of actually doing it. "You make me laugh. Not a lot of people can do that. Thank you."

"No, thank you. I had a wonderful afternoon."

"I had a wonderful time, too."

She reached in her large bag and pulled out a narrow box. "This is for you."

He smiled and nodded, not expecting the gift. "Thank you," he said. "Do I open it now?"

"No, later," she said. They got back to the car and headed to Serenity. They arrived twenty minutes later. He walked her back up to the penthouse then stopped at the door. "Aren't you coming in?" she asked hopefully.

"No, I have a few things to take care of. Tonight is the visual experience. Dinner this evening, I'll pick you up at eight. Dress to get my attention." She nodded and smiled. After shopping this morning she had a pretty good idea of what to wear.

Chapter 12

At seven forty-five Shay, wearing sheer stockings, extended her leg and fastened the last garter on her satin belt. She stood and slipped into her five-inch stiletto high heels then took one last look at her reflection in the dressing room's full-length mirror. She had to admit, the dress looked sensational. It was sexy, seductive and sophisticated. She remembered what Quinn had said earlier about attracting the man she wanted. Well, she knew exactly who she wanted to attract.

After trying on several of her new outfits, she chose the midnight-blue halter dress with matching fringed shawl. The dress was cut low and sexy. It was sleek and elegant with just a tantalizing hint of playfulness. It caressed and hugged her waist and hips perfectly then flared into a flirty full skirt that ended several playful inches above her knees.

The dress's generous low neckline exposed the tempting full swell of her breasts. She adjusted the neatly tied bow and took a deep breath to make sure it was securely fastened. It was. She turned around to look at the back of the dress in the mirror then turned to the front again. A single curled tendril of hair brushed atop her soft brown shoulder. She stepped closer and touched her already styled hair, pulling the strand up and pinning it into the French twist with a stylish comb she found in the boutique earlier. The end result was even more seductive and flattering than she expected. She certainly didn't look like the same woman who'd arrived here yesterday. She added scent and just a little makeup to complete the look. She smiled as she gazed at herself in the mirror and nodded her approval. "Perfect."

She spent the next few minutes reading through Quinn's book on seduction. She mentally checked off her progress. She'd gotten his attention. Now she needed to keep it. In the book he outlined several techniques. She chose the release method and decided to add her own spin to it.

A few minutes before eight o'clock, she paused a minute to calm her nerves. She draped her shawl across her shoulders and grabbed her purse then she opened the door and stepped out. She immediately heard soft music playing downstairs. She peeked over the second-floor balcony seeing Quinn dressed and standing at the window looking out. She smiled. Even from the back he looked gorgeous. She spared a moment to admire him unnoticed. He was cool and debonair. Then without provocation he turned around and looked up. He had on a dark blue suit, crisp white shirt and silver-gray tie. He smiled. “Hi,” she said as she walked the short length of the balcony then came downstairs.

“Hi,” he responded, walking toward the steps to wait.

When she got to the last few steps, she watched as he let his eyes drop down the full length of her body. His face seemed to light up. She’d obviously chosen the perfect outfit. “Hi,” she said again.

“Hi,” he repeated, holding his hand out to assist her on the last step. She stepped down. “You look stunning,” he said, holding her close.

“Thank you. You look pretty handsome yourself.” She reached out and lightly touched the tie she’d given him as a gift earlier. “I like the tie.”

He took her hand and kissed it, smiling. “Thank you, a friend gave it to me.”

She smiled. “It suits you.”

“I think so, too. Shall we?” he said, tipping his arm to her. “We have a brief stop to make before dinner.”

“Of course.” She adjusted the shawl on her shoulders. “I’m ready.”

They took the elevator to the lobby, passed through quickly and headed out to his car. She looked around for the sports convertible. It wasn’t there. “This way,” he said, touching the small of her back and guiding her a few steps toward a jet-black Mercedes-Benz sedan parked just to the side of the resort entrance.

"Nice car," she said.

"It seemed more apropos for the evening."

"So where's this brief stop we're making?" she asked.

"There's a private showing at a local art gallery. I thought you might like to join me," he said, opening the passenger side door for her.

"Sure, I'd love to." She got in and eased back into the rich black leather. She watched as he walked in front of the car and then got in. Moments later he pulled out and they drove down the hill toward Tucson. The streets were far less crowded than they had been earlier in the day.

In no time he pulled up in front of a large two-story building with an inset stone walkway. The valet immediately came over and opened her door. She got out and waited. Quinn took the ticket and escorted her down a narrow garden path through massive wooden doors that looked as if they'd been standing there since the beginning of time. Inside there was a large garden-style courtyard with guests already mingling.

The huge stone fountain in front instantly got her attention. It was old and weathered, but had a unique enduring quality. She stared a moment as did others. Then it hit her. The water seemed to flow upward defying gravity. She walked over for a closer look. It didn't of course, but the illusion was remarkable. Quinn followed. "Wow, this is so amazing. How do they do it?

It's kind of like the one at Serenity, but definitely not as modern and dramatic. But still…"

"You're right. This fountain dates back centuries, back since before the Mexican-American War. Nobody knows how or who created it or how long it's been here. They call it *la fuente del milagro del dios.* Translated loosely, it's called the source of God's miracle. The fountain at Serenity was styled and engineered by a sculptor using the same basic theory," he said. "I understand she studied the principles of this fountain for months before finding the solution."

"And what was the solution? How do you make running water appear to defy gravity?"

Quinn shook his head. "I have no idea. She's not talking."

"Smart lady, if I knew the secret I wouldn't tell, either." She stepped back to see the illusion effect. "It's so magical," she said. *"La fuente del milagro del dios."*

"It's told that soldiers from past wars used to bath in its water to heal their war wounds. It's the one place where there was never any fighting. Later the sick and ailing would come from all over just to touch the water. Some of the stones from the fountain itself date back several centuries before that. It's very mysterious and very magical.

"They say it just appeared overnight exactly as you see it. Then the building was constructed around it. It used to be an old Spanish monastery. There are still a number of catacombs and secret passages in the lower cellar. They were built to be crypts for monks." He leaned close and whispered, "But there were never any bodies interred."

Shay smiled, enjoying the stories. "It sounds fascinating," she said, looking around again. "It's old and it's still so beautiful."

"This whole area has an interesting history."

"I can imagine. So, have you bought art from this gallery?"

"Yes. I attend shows whenever I can. They usually have one-of-a-kind pieces. Tonight's show is a preview by invitation only. It'll open to the public next week." A waiter approached. Quinn took two glasses of champagne, handing her one. "To the perfect work of art," he said.

"Thank you," she said, then took a small sip and looked around again. "What's inside?"

"The main exhibit. Shall we?"

As they passed through the outer area several people walked over to greet him. He introduced Shay and they talked a moment than continued to the entrance. They walked up the stairs into the main gallery inside. There was a large painting just inside the doorway. Both stopped to examine it. Quinn leaned over to read the wall tag as others approached. Quinn stayed and talked as Shay moved on to the next piece. He shook hands and smiled dutifully as several of the guests complimented his work and began talking about their relationship experiences. He nodded appropriately and chuckled when expected. It was Publicity 101. He knew how to handle people.

After a particularly humorless story, he turned, spotting the blue dress instantly. His gaze drifted down the smooth silhouette of her appetizing body. The blue dress fit her perfectly. It molded to every sweeping curve in a mouthwatering waterfall of pure silk. Ending just a few playful inches above her knees, it was sexy and sophisticated. A slow burn began to simmer in his groin as he watched her move to another painting. For the first time he realized he wasn't the only one admiring her blue dress.

He saw the older man walk over and stand behind her. His eyes never left her body as he stepped closer and spoke. He watched Shay turn around and smile. They talked a moment then laughed then shook hands as he moved even closer. Quinn felt a tenseness in his body as his fists balled tightly and his brow arched. A muscle pulled tight in his jaw. There was something about the interaction he didn't like. Then he realized someone had asked him a question. Skillfully adept at evasion, he responded by tossing the question back to the asker who gleefully gave his opinion with righteous justification.

Surprisingly he had no idea what the conversation was about. More to the point, he didn't care. His thoughts had stayed on Shay. He watched her admiringly, as did most of the men in the room. There was no denying her beauty. She had a classic style and an exuberant energy that was unrivaled. Then, hoping to distract himself, he stepped away from the small gathering and began walking around the gallery, following her path. He spoke to several more guests, but always knew exactly where Shay was. The pieces might have been painted by da Vinci and sculpted by Michelangelo. He didn't know and he didn't care. The only work of art he saw was Shay.

Shay stopped at the next painting, tilted her head from side to side, then squinted her eyes hoping to see the significance of the piece. She didn't. It was a giant red dot with a massive dripping glob of metallic green paint beside it. There was also an eye and a nose coupled with an orange mushroom painted in pointillism. She shook her head and chucked to herself, thinking the artist had had one too many. Nothing about this work impressed her. Each piece was more outrageous than the last, and not in a good way.

"So, what do you think of the work?" She heard asked over her shoulder. She turned around seeing an older man standing behind her. He looked close to seventy or so. He had large white teeth and small narrow glasses. He was elegantly dressed in a chocolate-colored velvet jacket and paisley designed ascot and carried an ivory cane which she suspected was more for style than necessity. She smiled politely. "I haven't seen the entire show yet."

"Ahhh, but your first impression is usually the right one and certainly the most honest. So, tell me, what do you think?"

"Are you the artist?" she asked.

He chuckled then answered. “No.”

“Good, then in my opinion his work seems scattered. He’s experimenting with too many styles and techniques on the same canvas. There’s pointillism, impressionism, cubism and even baroque. Maybe if he just focused on one. What about you, what do you think?”

“Absolutely stunning,” he said, looking at her rather than the work.

“If you say so,” she yielded.

He moved closer and spoke near her ear. “Actually, my dear, I was talking about you.”

She smiled and nodded. “Thank you.”

“By the way, you’re right about the art. It’s crap,” he said. Shay laughed, taken off guard by the flippant remark. “You are stunning. I’d love to take you to my studio and show you my work, possibly even paint you,” he said.

“Now that’s a line I haven’t heard in a while,” she joked.

He laughed loud. “I like that, refreshingly honest. The name’s Ham McBride,” he said, introducing himself while extending his hand to shake.

“Shay Daniels. Nice to meet you.” She shook his hand.

“Shay, that’s a beautiful name.” He held on to her hand as he talked. “So Shay, what do you think about coming to my studio and allowing me to sketch you? I promise to be on my best behavior.”

“Are you flirting with me, Ham?”

“I certainly hope so,” he said, smiling wickedly.

She chuckled. “Well, Ham, even though I’m sure you would be on your best behavior, I’m going to very graciously decline.”

“More’s the pity.” He reached into his pocket and handed her his card. “Perhaps you’ll reconsider. Think about it.”

“Perhaps, but not today. It was nice meeting you.”

“Likewise, my dear, likewise.” Still holding her hand he kissed it and winked. “Do think about it.”

He walked away and an instant later Quinn walked up. “Are you enjoying yourself?”

“Yes, I am.”

“I think we’ve put in enough of an appearance. Are you ready to go?”

“Sure.”

Moments later the valet pulled the car up and they got in. “That was great. I really enjoyed myself. I still can’t believe the fountain. It’s so amazing.”

“What did you think of the art?”

“Not exactly a fan. It was a bit out there for me. I prefer the simple expression of art. Did you buy anything?”

“No, not this time,” he said.

“So, where’s dinner?” she asked.

“It’s a nice quiet place not too far from the resort. Sit back and relax, we’ll be there in a few minutes.”

Shay looked out the side window seeing the last sights of the city disappear in the distance. They continued out past the city limits into complete darkness. Safe and secure, she felt at ease in the car with Quinn. It was like they were the only two people on the planet. Shay rested her head back and closed her eyes. The soothing hum of the engine lulled her. When she opened her eyes Quinn had turned off the main highway and onto a side street then a secluded road. Moments later he pulled up in front of a gorgeous structure then circled around to the side.

She glanced up. There were two other cars in the open space in front. One she recognized instantly. It was Quinn's silver sports car from that afternoon. She turned to him. "Your home?"

He nodded. "Dinner should be just about ready." He parked and got out and walked around to the passenger side to open the door for her. Shay got out, looking around. His home was nothing like she imagined. It was huge and ultra modern, but still classic. It was well lit and completely surrounded in darkness. He took her hand and they walked along the white slate path to the front door. He opened it. She went inside and he followed.

The motion sensor lights turned on automatically. She looked around the massive inside area. It was a great room connecting the living room, dining room and kitchen. The ceiling had to be nearly twenty-five feet high. Everything was perfect. It looked like it was torn from an architectural magazine layout. It was elegantly furnished, styled perfectly for a man alone. The foyer area was set up two steps higher than the rest of the area. She stepped down, walked around the living room and turned. Quinn was still standing near the front door watching her. "What do you think?" he asked.

She nodded, turning around in a complete circle then back to face him. "It's gorgeous."

"I'm glad you like it. I hoped you would."

"Why is that?" she asked casually.

"You're the first woman to see it. I've never brought anyone here before."

"I'm glad," she said. Then, for the first time that evening, she let the silken shawl drop from her shoulders. She tossed it on one of the plush sofas and turned away. She knew exactly what she was doing. The backless dress was a showstopper. She could almost hear his jaw hit the floor. She didn't have to turn around to know that his eyes were probably glazed over.

Quinn knew exactly where she'd gotten the idea of adding a pleasurable surprise element to a seduction. It was from his book. And, this was certainly a pleasant surprise. "Can I get you something to drink?" he asked, feeling the familiar tightness in his groin again.

She turned and looked at him then nodded slowly. "Yes, a glass of wine would be nice."

He nodded then walked over to the open kitchen area and stood at the back counter a moment to get himself together. She was getting to him and using his own words to do it. He removed his suit jacket and loosened his tie. Then after a few deep breaths he went to the front counter overlooking the open area.

There were already two glasses and a bottle of wine left out for them. He uncorked and poured the wine into the glasses then watched as Shay continued walking around the living room. She stopped in front of the large fireplace. There was an antique turnstile arm and covered pot over the logs. She looked back at him. "I don't suppose you cook dinner using this," she joked.

He smiled. "No, not often," he assured her.

She nodded then reached over and opened the lid. Seeing it was empty, she replaced it and looked up at the mantel. It was sparsely decorated with candles, an antique box, two small sculptures and a photograph. Quinn watched as she picked up the photo and held it closer. She smiled and turned to him as he approached with the glasses. "Is this your mom and dad?"

"Yes, it's the only picture I have of us all together."

"Is this your wife?" she asked, seeing the smiling woman posed next to him.

He handed her a glass of wine. "Yes."

"She was beautiful."

"Yes, she was."

"What was she like?" she asked, setting the photo back down and taking a sip of wine.

"She was smart, strong-willed, restless, outgoing."

"She sounds like fun."

"She had her moments," he said softly.

"So, you said that you didn't date a lot. Is that because you're looking for someone to measure up to her, or to try to replace her?" she asked.

"What makes you ask that?" he said tightly.

"You said before that you hadn't had a real relationship

in a long time. Maybe it's because you're still holding on to your wife."

"Believe me, I'm not holding on to anything or anyone and I certainly know no one will ever replace her."

His last words struck hard. Shay felt like knives had pierced her heart. It was obvious he was still in love with his wife. She took a step back. His denial was more forceful than she expected. Everything about him suddenly changed. A massive wall of pain seemed to separate them. "I'm sorry. I didn't mean to bring up painful memories. I guess I was just curious about her."

"Don't be," he said defensively.

"Look, I understand. I really understand," she said softly, taking another step back. "You never really get over the first time you really fall in love."

"No, you don't understand."

"So, I guess that kind of dampens the mood, huh?"

"It's not what you think," he said, putting his glass down and taking her hand. He looked into her soft brown eyes. Suddenly his throat went dry. A feeling of need swept over him. But it wasn't the physical need, although that was certainly there. He wanted her. There was no denying that fact. But there was more. He wanted what she did for him. He felt a sense of completeness when she was around. "Right now, Shay, you are the woman I'm thinking about."

Quinn felt the words seep deeper into his heart even more than he expected. In truth, she was the only woman he thought about and it had nothing to do with his work.

He knew right then, that instant, that she was the one. She was nothing like anyone he'd met before. Her joyous spirit swept over him and seemed to stimulate a part of him he'd long since buried and forgotten.

Shay looked into his eyes. She knew he was telling at least part of the truth. But she also knew that the "right now" part wouldn't last and there was no way she was going to put her heart on the line for something she knew wouldn't last. She'd done that too many times before. She tried to remind herself that this was just about the physical. The attraction was mutual and the need to satisfy that hunger they both felt was the only thing between them.

She smiled, seeing his warmth and sincerity. But she also saw something else. There was struggle in his eyes. Perhaps this was too fast and too soon. "You know what? I think maybe this is going too fast for you. It's like you said, hearts heal in their own time. I think I should go. I'll wait for you outside." She set the glass down, grabbed her shawl and headed back to the front door.

He followed. "Shay," he called out.

She got to the door, opened it and then faced him. "I'm sorry," she said, and then turned to leave.

Chapter 13

Shay took two steps outside the door then felt Quinn grab her hand and hold tight. She stopped. It was obvious she wasn't going anywhere. He turned her around and pulled her flush against the solidness of his body. The sudden jolt took her breath away. She gasped, immediately feeling his hardness pressed to her as he sandwiched her between his body and the door frame. She felt her insides gel. She looked up into his dark stormy eyes as he leaned close. Then, just inches away, he paused and whispered two words. "Please stay."

She opened her mouth to speak, but in one smooth swift motion, he cupped and angled her head to meet his. The kiss was instant and his tongue delved deep as soon as their lips touched. She surrendered, wrapping her arms around his neck and holding tight. She felt a seething surge of passion erupt throughout her body. She tingled everywhere. It had been too long and right now she never wanted this feeling to end. As the kiss deepened she pressed closer and pulled harder, molding her body to his as much as she possibly could. Being closer to him was all she could fathom.

He kissed her neck, nibbling down and across her shoulder. Her breathing was ragged and halting. She dug her nails into his shoulder, gripping tight, wanting as much of him as she could get. Weak and breathless, she rolled her neck back as his kisses became more intense and passionate. She wanted to give him everything, all of her all at once. They were ravenous, kissing, touching, caressing, stroking. Then just as quickly the heated passion subsided to a slow sultry sizzle. He teased her with his mouth as his hands burned right through her dress. She leaned back against the door again, letting him do as he pleased, and he pleased her so very well.

When the kiss finally ended they just stood there in the open doorway staring. She nibbled at her swollen lower lip. He reached up and touched it. "Did I hurt you?" he asked, concerned.

"No, not at all," she said.

"It's not what you think. I don't want to replace my wife ever. My life with her was over a long time ago. I have long since closed that chapter in my life." His eyes begged her understanding. "Please stay," he repeated.

Shay nodded her head. Was he kidding? After that, wild horses couldn't drive her away. "Yes," she said.

He took her hand and guided her back inside. He closed the door and leaned close, trapping her with his body again. Neither spoke a word. She reached up and touched his chest, feeling that his heart was pounding and beating as fast as hers. She looked into his soulful eyes. His expression was unmistakable and she knew at this moment he would surrender to whatever she wanted.

With her hand still on his chest, she moved him to take a step back. She needed to feel more of him. She ran her hands down his chest to his abs and stomach. She felt already tightened muscles clinch harder then relax. The physical effect she was having on him made her want even more. She touched his neck, his shoulders, his arms, his waist and then she inched lower. The solid outline of his penis made her tremble inside. He was hard, long and thick. Her mouth went dry instantly as she stroked down the length of him then eased back up. She licked her lips, ready for more when her shawl, still on her shoulders, dropped to her hand, getting in the way.

He stilled her hand and slowly removed her shawl and tossed it on the cushioned chair by the door. She was breathless with anticipation, wanting to touch more of him. Her heart fluttered and pounded thunderously. The look in his eyes was pure passion. Still holding her hand, he backed her up against the door again. He looked down the full length of her body. Her breathing quickened.

She opened her mouth to speak, but only gasped. He

touched her, running a finger down the side of her jaw, then down her neck to the low plunge of her dress.

She closed her eyes and licked her lips. He had only used two fingers and already she was on fire. She couldn't imagine anything simpler, yet he was sending shock waves through her body. Then he continued down to the flat of her stomach, across her pelvis and down her thigh. He slowly pulled the hem of her dress up feeling the sheer stocking along the way. When he got to the satin garter belt he stopped. She opened her eyes, smiled. Another surprise. Looking at him, it was obvious he hadn't expected that. Still he was staring straight at her with a sexy half smile she knew too well. He obviously liked surprises.

He leaned in and kissed her slowly, taking his time teasing her lips and dipping his tongue torturously into her mouth. She tried to force a more intense kiss, but he backed away each time. The playful interaction only intensified her desire for him. He nuzzled and kissed her neck as his hand continued to explore her body. He reached behind and grabbed her rear, squeezing and pressing her even closer. Her body trembled and her legs weakened. She wanted him now, but she knew he was nowhere near done.

He leaned back. She saw the desire in her eyes reflected in his. In a split second he whisked her up in his arms. He kissed her neck and shoulder as she snuggled close. This was more than she ever imagined. She wrapped her arms around his neck and held tight as he carried her away. She didn't know where they were going, she didn't care. All she knew was that she was with the man she was falling in love with.

After a few minutes he gently released her, letting her slowly slide down the length of his body. She looked around. They were standing in the threshold of his bedroom. She turned to him and reached up to touch the smooth surface of his face. Then she grabbed one end of his loosened tie, undid the perfect knot and guided him inside. By the time the tie's other end was completely freed from his neck she was standing right beside his big bed. He grabbed and held the other end just before it slipped from around his neck. Smiling, she slowly began pulling the tie knowing he'd wouldn't let go. When she had gathered it, they were standing face-to-face. She slipped the last end from his fingers and tossed it on the bed. Then she unbuttoned his shirt and pulled it away, tossing it near the tie.

She smiled. His chest was magnificent. She ran her hands over his shoulders and chest then drifted down to his waistband and pulled him close. She leaned up and kissed his neck. "Unzip me," she whispered, and then turned around. She slowly untied the halter bow as he pulled the dress's zipper down. She let it drop and stepped out. He bent down to pick it up just as she turned around again. He stopped midway. The dress slipped from his fingers. She smiled knowingly. Obviously he liked what he saw. "Maybe you should sit down," she said playfully.

"Good idea." He nodded and took a step back, sitting on the side of the bed. But to her surprise he pulled her with him to fit perfectly between his long legs. She stood in satin panties, lace garter, sheer stockings and stilettos. "Oh yeah, this is pure seduction," he said, admiring her less than modest attire. Her perky full breasts and her pebbled nipples beckoned straight ahead. They were exactly his eye level. He sat speechless as his gaze never left her body.

He reached up and brushed his finger against a taut nipple. She inched back as an instant ripple shot through her. He smiled, seeing her reaction and moved to hold her in place. He touched her again. The same tingle shot through, but this time he held her in place. "That tickles," she said.

"Then how about this," he offered. With his hands still on her waist he pulled her forward. He opened his mouth and licked the brown orb surrounding her nipple. Breathless, she shivered. He licked the other nipple and ardently savored the sweet mouthful. Her legs weakened. It was the most intense pleasure-pain she'd ever felt. Soon the exquisite sensation of his mastery began.

She held tight to his shoulders, arching forward to the simple pull of his mouth. Each tantalizing lick of his tongue and suckle of his mouth sent a ripple of tingles through her body. It was too much and not nearly enough. He placed his hands on her rounded apple-bottom cheeks and pulled her forward as his mouth continued the stimulating assault. She was wet and ready for him now. "Quinn, I need you inside of me. Make love to me, now."

"Patience, my sweet, we have all night. And I intend to use every second of it."

She leaned down, cupping his face with her hands and kissed him tenderly. Over and over and over again, their lips met, their tongues tasted and their mouths consumed the other. More and more the kiss took them as arousal pushed them further to the edge. A sudden fierceness of passion took control. The need was too great, the desire was too intense. They were getting beyond carried away. Every nerve ending in her body sizzled and her stomach did somersaults. He pulled her closer. She climbed up and straddled his lap, feeling the steel rod of his erection beneath her.

Instantly their savory kisses exploded in a barrage of slow, sensuous passion. She gyrated her hips while on his lap and felt his body stiffen. The slow movement excited him. She leaned back and stood to remove the rest of her clothes. She carefully placed her foot on his thigh. He removed one shoe then the other. She unsnapped the front garter then turned and backed up. He rubbed the flat of his palms on her bottom and down the length of her legs. Then he unsnapped her satin garters and slowly eased her stocking down her legs.

She turned back to him and pulled his hand until he stood. He knew it was his turn. He unzipped his pants and let them fall to the floor. Then he removed his boxer-briefs and she nearly stopped breathing. He reached over and grabbed condoms from the nightstand. He covered himself then sat, guiding her back between his legs. He circled the lace band of her panties and slowly eased them down her body. He guided her to turn and sit back on his lap.

He felt, caressed, stroked and massaged her body everywhere. She arched back as his one hand covered her breast as the other toyed torturously between her legs. This was just like her fantasy. She gasped and instinctively closed her legs. "Open," he whispered. She didn't hear him at first. The thought of what he wanted to do to her already had her mind in a twisted haze. "Open for me," he said.

"Quinn, I…I…" she muttered, still in her rapturous haze.

"Shhh…open." He eased her legs apart, letting each drop to the side of his. An instant later he found *that* spot. His fingers delved inside as his thumb teased the tiny nub. Her body trembled then she gyrated, moving her hips to the sweet feel of his hand on her. She moved faster, closing her eyes tight and opening her mouth, breathing hard and heavy. She felt her body tense and her orgasm near release. Seconds later she shrieked and writhed as pleasure shot through her over and over again. She gasped as her body trembled and shook, taking each thrusting spasm higher and higher. She came again and again, his hands still on her. Then she stilled his hands and lay back against his chest, willing her body to come down.

She slid around him and lay back on the bed cushioned by the thick soft pillows around her. He came to her hovering just above her body. She reached up to him, smiling. "Come inside," she whispered, wanting to feel the fullness of him inside of her now. He leaned down capturing her lips then trailing kisses and nibbles down her neck and shoulders, to her chest and stomach. She watched and waited as he lavished her body with his mouth then repeated the action with his hand. She quivered as his fingers twirled and teased her all over again.

An instant later he took both her hands and raised them up above her head and held them secure. Then he dipped his body down to her. She felt the steel hardness of his penis tease between her legs. She arched her body up to meet him and wrapped her legs around his waist. He entered in one smooth swift thrust of passion.

She shrieked and gasped as her body trembled. She was tight. "Are you okay?" he asked.

She nodded. "Oh, yes, perfect."

He began to move. The rhythm of his body easily synced with hers. She began grinding her hips as he delved in. The rhythm picked up instantly as they met power for power. Sensual and passionate, the slow tension built into a fury of ecstasy as rapturous delight became a throbbing, thrusting, stoking abandonment of passion.

She held tight, her hands roamed his back and held his waist, feeling the power of his body surging into hers. He filled and refilled her body, deeper and deeper each stroke brought them closer and closer. Their heaving ragged breaths mingled with unrestrained control. The tempo increased then slowed as wave after wave they surrendered as one.

In amorous excitement she dug her nails into his shoulders as her climax swept over her again. She cried out but the sound was instantly swallowed by his kiss. Again and again the dance accelerated to pounding fury, a force beyond what either expected. They thrust, surging faster and faster as frantic tension drove them higher and higher. Then in a crescendo of pure exhilaration the moment of ecstasy took them. Their climax erupted and they pinnacled in the sated fulfillment of desire.

Breathless, Quinn rolled over quickly taking her to his side and holding her close. He stroked her back lovingly and kissed her temple. "Hey, how are you?" he asked.

Shay sighed in luxurious wonder. "I am simply divine. What about you?"

He smiled to himself. "I'm fantastic."

"You certainly are. So, Doc, what's my next lesson?"

"I don't think you need lessons from me anymore. You've just gone to the head of the class."

"Wow, I guess the makes me valedictorian." She giggled and wiggled her butt, grinding against him.

He covered her breasts, pressing his body even closer and began kissing her neck and shoulder. "Are you trying to get me started again?" She giggled, wiggling more. His arousal level was just about ready to shoot through the roof. He took a deep breath and exhaled slowly. "You know, we never did eat dinner. Are you hungry?"

"Yeah, but later," she hummed, as she cuddled closer and closed her eyes. He held her tighter and her thoughts wandered. This was what lovemaking should feel like all the time; the closeness, the tenderness, the bonding and the passion. Every fiber of her being was energized and relaxed all at the same time. How she could have missed out on this feeling for so long was beyond her. No one had ever made her feel like this. She took a deep contented breath then exhaled slowly. “Don’t let me fall asleep,” she whispered as she happily drifted off.

Quinn’s heartbeat returned to its normal rhythm and the tenseness in his body had long since subsided. He looked down at Shay. The thought of the pleasure he’d just experienced made his body want her all over again. At thirty-five years old, he’d never felt this connected with anyone ever before. He leaned down and kissed her forehead tenderly, hearing the slow even sound of her breathing. He closed his eyes just for a minute. Moments later they were both asleep in each other’s arm.

An hour later, Quinn opened his eyes to find Shay lying there by his side. They had both fallen asleep. He liked that. He looked down at her now. Her face was placid and she looked perfect lying there beside him. He watched as she breathed slowly. The sweet swell of her breasts rose and fell with each inhale and exhale. His body instantly reacted as want and desire quickly surged. He stoked the length of her back gently. Waking up with her by his side could definitely become a nice habit. He touched the soft outline around her face, definitely a nice habit.

He smiled, remembering them making love just an hour earlier. Their bodies had fit together perfectly. It was like they'd known each other forever. He liked the feeling. She was open and creative and made his body burn just standing there. Even now, just thinking about her, made him want her.

She stirred. He looked down. The sheet shifted, exposing her breast. He smiled and licked his lips, remembering the feel of her in his mouth and on his tongue. She was firm and hard and he liked the way she moaned and shuddered when he tasted her.

His hunger for her was returning fast. He realized he needed to get up now. He eased away, got up and looked back at her sleeping. The silhouette of her perfect form enticed him again. He walked away quickly.

He washed up, then went down to the kitchen and checked the refrigerator for the dinner he had prepared for them earlier. He found the containers and detailed instructions on reheating the meal. He followed the directions and in twenty minutes everything was piping hot and ready to be served.

He grabbed a large tray, loaded it with everything he needed then took it back upstairs to his bedroom. Shay, having rolled over on her stomach, was still asleep. He took the tray and set the meal up out on the terrace. When everything was set he went back in and sat down on the side of the bed. Shay stirred, rolled to her side to face him, and then gazed up at him, smiling. She looked enticingly inviting. "Hey," she said seductively, her voice was huskier and sexier than usual.

"Hey, right back," he said, running his hand along

the silhouette of her half-covered form. He got to her rear and squeezed gently.

She moaned then took a deep breath and stretched. The sheet covering her breasts dipped just low enough to hint at her naked body beneath. "What time is it?" she asked.

"Time to eat," he said, trying to control the surging need to bury himself between her legs.

"You have food for me?" she asked. He nodded. She stretched again and this time rolled back onto her stomach.

He pulled the sheet down and stroked her back, ending on her rear again. He leaned down and kissed her neck, shoulders and back, tempting her with each kiss and more. "Caesar salad, chicken Marseilles with smashed red skin potatoes and grilled asparagus and for dessert, tiramisu."

"Umm…yum…I'm up."

Fifteen minutes later they were sitting out on the terrace well into the best chicken Marseilles with smashed red skin potatoes and grilled asparagus she'd ever had. They talked and laughed reminiscing about the art show that evening.

"Please give my compliments to the chef."

"I certainly will."

"Well, I guess I'd better get back to the resort."

"You don't have to."

"Yes, I do. There's no way I'm going to do the walk of shame through a crowded lobby at nine in the morning wearing the same outfit I had on the night before."

"Walk of shame?" he questioned.

"It's a chick term," she assured him. "It means being out all night and trying to sneak in the next morning like nothing happened." He laughed.

For the next hour and a half they sat out on the terrace eating tiramisu and talking about psychology. It was well past midnight when he finally drove her back to the resort. They waved at Carlos as they headed to the elevator and up to the penthouse. When the doors opened she stepped out, took a few steps and turned, realizing he wasn't behind her. He pressed the hold button. "Aren't you coming in?" she asked.

He shook his head. "No, I need to be away from the resort. I have to get some work done and take care of some business."

She nodded, trying not to look as disappointed as she felt. "Okay, I'll see you when you get back."

"It might be a few days." He rolled his finger, motioning for her to come closer. She did. He wrapped his arm around her waist and pulled her close nuzzling her neck. "You are magnificent," he whispered. His warm breath on her neck made her shiver.

"Yeah, I get that a lot." He leaned back and kissed her long and lavishly. It was meant to seal a night of passion. When the kiss began to deepen she took a step back. "Goodbye," she said.

"Good night." He released the button and the doors closed in slow motion.

They stood looking into each other's eyes until the doors completely closed. Shay stood a moment longer hoping he'd press the button and come back, but he didn't. After a while she turned and went up to her room. It was the best first and last date she had ever had. She knew a dumping when she saw it. Quinn was dumping her. But to his credit it was the best she'd ever had.

Chapter 14

The day after they'd made love, Shay had stayed in the sensuous afterglow of their evening all morning long. The passion, hunger and desire made it seem like it had just happened moments earlier. Her senses were still tuned to him and she felt the stir of being with him. She had stayed in bed until noon. When she finally got up she lounged around the penthouse, read two of his books, swam in the balcony pool and then lay out in the sun until it slowly set behind the mountains.

Saying she missed him out loud was absurd. How could she miss him when she really didn't even know him? He was exactly what she planned, a vacation fling. That was her solace and justification for shutting down all day. She'd had her pleasure and now it was over. He told her he'd be away and she knew he was gone, but still a part of her hoped he would appear. He didn't.

Now, two days later, a brilliant dawn barely broke through the sky as Shay opened her eyes. Just like yesterday, she didn't move after waking up. She just lay in bed thinking and remembering. The first forty-eight hours of her vacation had been a whirlwind of excitement. She had never been so happy and felt so much pleasure. As she had promised herself, she went out, found a gorgeous man and had her world rocked.

Quinn was amazing. Being with him had changed so many things. Now she was sure, certain without a shadow of doubt that there was such a thing as romance. He had certainly romanced her. In that short time they were together she couldn't ever remember being so happy. From the first instant she saw him she felt something different. It was a kind of inner peace and anticipation and a connection she couldn't explain. But it was there.

He had touched every part of her, emotionally, physically and spiritually. He was everything any woman could want or ask for in a man. She now knew why his nickname was Dr. Love. He was that and so much more. But never in a million years did she think she'd fall in love with him—yet she had. It was easy. She just hoped falling out would be just as painless. But already her heart ached in a way that she never thought it could.

She loved him. She looked up at the ceiling trying to pinpoint the moment she felt it, but couldn't. It seemed like it was always there. Like the first moment she turned and saw him outside the forum, it was there. Everything after that was the buildup of a lasting bonding. Whenever or why ever it happened, she knew she felt it. It was just like he said, theia mania, love at first sight.

She closed her eyes. Of course she dreamed about him. How could she not? They had come together in a night of passion that she would remember for the rest of her life. Even now his kisses still burned across her body. The pull of his mouth and touch of his hands would forever be a part of her.

It was like a dream or in this case a fantasy. Their lovemaking was epic. Their bodies moved on one accord, fitting together perfectly. Every touch, every kiss and every stroke sent shivers of delight through her body. Then when she reached her climax, it was like the world exploded and they were the only two people left. She sighed dreamily. But she knew she needed to resolve herself that she was the only one feeling this. She knew it was merely a physical attraction and release as far was Quinn was concerned. She could never have anything more than that night and the love she felt in her heart. It could never be returned. She'd seen the pain and anguish in his eyes when they talked about his wife's death. She knew exactly what it was. He was still in love with her.

She opened her eyes suddenly. The idea came to her out of the blue. The interview Jade wanted her to write about Quinn wasn't going to happen. But she did want to write a series of articles about her experiences at the resort. She was on a love high and she wanted to spread the word. She was going to talk to Jade about doing a series type article in the online magazine. It would be the perfect accent to the show. She'd tape a show and then write the article and have a blog forum to let others participate. They could write reviews and post comments about their experiences at the particular location. It was the perfect format to spark some energy back into the show.

She sat up, grabbed her laptop and began writing the first article, careful not to be too specific about Quinn and to only relay her opinions and not state any direct quotes or conversations. This wasn't his interview. It was hers. She wrote a list of questions she needed to have answered about Serenity and the surrounding area. The questions turned into guidelines which quickly turned into a whole new idea about dating and romantic relationships. The kernel of an idea was taking on a life of its own and she excitedly ran with it.

Two hours later, her energy levels were through the roof and she needed to run. She needed a release and running was always it. She got up, grabbed a quick shower and called down to the guest services for assistance. Thankfully, Alona picked up. They spoke a while then Shay told her what she wanted. Alona gave her several options according to what she was interesting in doing. Shay told her she wanted to see the top of the world or in this case the Tucson area. Alona narrowed it down to a single trail that sounded perfect. She also suggested a walk instead of running and to carry a lightweight backpack. She agreed and asked about purchasing one. Alona promised to have one packed and ready at guest services when she came down.

Excitedly Shay put on her shorts, T-shirt and sneakers and headed downstairs. Everything was set up on the counter when she got there. "Good morning," Shay said, seeing Alona checking over supplies.

Alona looked up, smiling. "Good morning. Are you ready?"

"Yes," she said, moving to the counter to see everything Alona pulled out for her.

"Okay, the most important thing about hiking in the mountains is staying on the paths. They're there for a reason. I know you might be tempted to veer off, but don't do it. It's dangerous."

"Dangerous how? Snakes and coyotes and things?" she asked.

"Yes, but more likely loose rocks. It's very easy to slip and fall and you need to be careful even on the trails. Now here's your map. I've highlighted several different trails you can take including one that's very scenic and very high. They're all very enjoyable."

Shay nodded. "Good, okay. What's all this?"

"Backpack supplies," she said, picking each up and storing it in the pack. "Two bottles of water, bug spray, antiseptic with bandages, an extra map in plastic, granola and protein bars, beef jerky, whistle and a flashlight." She zipped the bag. "There, you're all set."

"Alona, I'm only gonna be gone for a few hours."

"You're going into the desert, you need to be prepared. What you really need is a hiking partner."

"Alona, I'll be fine. I'm sure there will be others on the trail."

Alona nodded hesitantly, but still instructed Shay on step-by-step procedure in case anything happened and again reminded her to stay on the marked path. Moments later Shay was all set. With her map in hand, Alona walked her outside and pointed her in the right direction then gave her a general idea of what to expect. A few minutes later Shay was on her way.

She found the path at the foothills of a small valley without any problem. There were already several people walking and running the trail, so she stretched and joined them. The first few miles were quick and easy. The road was flat and paved and not at all as difficult as she thought it might be. The paths were readily marked along the way. At several points there were varying directions to take. Since she always chose the high road and the path of most resistance, she got off the flat paved road and chose another.

Going the easy way wasn't in her nature and this certainly wasn't a leisurely Sunday afternoon nature walk. The ground terrain quickly changed from paved to gravel and then to a sand/stone mix. The impact was slightly cushioned, but still rough. The walk was getting to be more grueling and with slipping, near treacherous at times. But it was also the most invigorating and exhilarating walk she had taken in a long time. There was another path split. She chose the more upward direction.

At this point she climbed a steep incline basically walking in a side step motion. It circled the lower hill then jetted straight up the back side of another upward plateau. When she reached the leveled site she stopped, turned and looked back. She was amazed at how far she'd come in such a short time. Even though it was still early morning, and a thick haze settled like a blanket, she could plainly see the resort in the far distance and the city of Tucson even farther away. The city seemed to sit in a pocket surrounded by four other very distinct mountain ranges.

She opened the backpack and grabbed one of the water bottles Alona packed. She was right, running would have been too grueling and she wasn't used to the Arizona climate. But mostly, she definitely needed a backpack. She sipped from the bottled water and stood catching her breath. It was already warm when she started, so by the time she climbed the hills the temperature had seemed to climb with her. The morning heat had descended on the valley like a solar flare. But there was no way she'd have missed this sight. It was absolutely spectacular.

She couldn't even imagine being back in New York right now, the traffic, the crowds and the craziness. She loved her city, but being here right now was like sitting on top of the world all alone. She smiled thinking about the past few days. Nothing about this place was what she expected and certainly not Quinn.

She turned back and looked up, spotting another plateau a lot higher up. But going forward would mean a harder climb and a much more dangerous descent. The choice was easy and the decision was quick. She walked and climbed.

Twenty minutes later she reached that plateau and looked up higher still. There was no way she'd go higher. This was as close to the top as she could come. Panting hard, she sat and drank the rest of the first water bottle as she stayed there just looking down at the remarkable view. She pulled out her notebook and began jotting down notes and feelings for the article she intended to write.

Then she pulled out her phone and took pictures to send to Jade. She sat on a rock and soaked in the peace and serenity around her. After a while she stood preparing to walk down. Her cell phone rang. It was Jade. Smiling, she picked up. "Hey, did you see the pictures I just sent? Can you believe this view?"

"Hey," Jade said, slightly less enthused than she expected. "Yeah, the pictures are beautiful. I just saw them. Where are you?"

Shay smiled and looked around shaking her head in awe and wonder. "I'm on top of the world, almost literally. It's amazing here. The haze has lifted and I can see almost forever. The pictures are beautiful, but actually being here is amazing. I could seriously stay here forever."

"Yes, I like them. They're really nice, but umm..." Jade said then trailed off, stalling.

"What's going on? What's up?" Shay asked, once deliriously happy, but now suddenly concerned.

Jade hesitated then dived in. "I was in meetings all morning. As editor-in-chief of the magazine I just got my promo advertising for next season's cable shows. *Romantic Destinations* isn't listed. I found out later it's going to be cancelled."

An icy chill shot through Shay's body. "Cancelled?"

"Yes, cancelled. I shouldn't be telling you this because the programming schedule hasn't been finalized. The network is cancelling the show to make room for two others."

"What! No!" Shay said, as she sat down slowly feeling like her world had just shattered into a million pieces. "But our ratings are still good. Granted, we had an off season, but I can get them back up. We've been the network's most watched show for three years in a row. Last season was the only time we didn't make the top of the list."

"One slow season is all it takes sometimes. You know that."

"Still, why would they just cancel us?"

"The reason is simple, economics, why else? They think they can do it cheaper. Right now there are two treatments in the works. The network is doing a more infomercial type show. In that one the initial plan is for the resorts to furnish their own tapes for broadcast on the network. The other is to hire a sexier host to generate more heat. The premise is a more reality TV format.

Either choice, in their eyes, it's a win-win situation for them."

"I can't believe this," Shay said, still shocked by the real possibility of her show's demise.

"Believe it, it's true. If ever you need a miracle you need one now. You need to get Dr. Love to maybe do a season with you. That would definitely change their minds."

"He doesn't do that anymore."

"Talk him into it."

"And how am I supposed to do that?"

"You know that famous line, 'by any means necessary?' Well that's exactly it. Wine him, dine him, beg him, seduce him, whatever it takes. You want to have a job in six weeks and finally become executive producer of your own show. This is definitely the step in that direction. You gotta make it happen, Shay. I gotta go. Call me later, okay."

Shay ended the call, but stood in shock. So much for the peaceful escape from craziness. Just when she thought everything was coming together in her life, this happened. She tried to call Jade back, but couldn't get a signal. She turned around in several directions. There was no signal reception on top of the mountain.

Shay started down the mountain. Each step became more purposeful. She needed to find out exactly what was going on in New York. She slipped then caught herself and kept going. By the time she was halfway down, she saw what looked like a shortcut off the main trail. It could probably cut her walk down by fifteen or twenty minutes. She decided to take it even though Alona made her promise to stay on the trail.

The shortcut was harder than it looked and a lot more treacherous, but she continued. She slipped again and this time barely caught herself in time. She grabbed a bush to steady herself, but the bush quickly gave way and something that looked like a snake slithered near. She jumped back, slipped and tumbled. This time she didn't catch herself and there was nothing to hold on to but thin air. The last thing she saw was a cloud of dust and the top of the mountain getting farther and farther away.

After leaving Shay, Quinn got in the elevator and headed down to the lobby. When the doors opened he couldn't move. His body tried, but his heart wouldn't let him. One night wasn't enough. He had a feeling it was never going to be enough. He pressed the button to go back up, but didn't insert his key card. The elevator reached the top floor, but wouldn't go any higher without the room card. He pulled it out to insert it, and then stopped. He realized the feelings he was experiencing. It was what he'd been hoping would happen, but to his astonishment, it was happening to him instead. He pressed the lobby button again. This time when the doors opened he walked out.

He went back to his house and worked all night. Although it wasn't what he expected, he had exactly what he needed—firsthand knowledge. The feelings and emotions were his. Their night together had confirmed what he already knew in his heart. It was the perfect ending to his study. Afterward he went back and reexamined his previous research. He needed to make a lot of changes.

The next day he was absorbed in making corrections and revisions. He challenged his own findings, things he'd always took as fact. Everything he thought his study was about was the exact opposite. He'd just stayed up all night when Nola called early the following morning. She had yet another promotional plan. This time it was about the Sonora Equinox Party.

"Quinn, you have to publicize it nationally. Imagine how much more money you'll bring in. A few interviews is all it'll take, trust me."

"Nola, you know I'm done with interviews and all that."

"Quinn, think about it. This is a golden opportunity. It's a small step. We can't let this one pass. What if I set up very specific interviews, nothing too big?"

"No. No interviews."

"Quinn, you're wasting my time if all you want for me to do is organize your book signings, maintain your website and keep you out of the tabloids. Technically it's my job to keep you in the news. I can set up an interview with a small publication and then something national for your foundation."

She hit him where he was most susceptible, his foundation. "Okay, okay, fine, one local interview and one national one."

"Yes, you won't be sorry," she said quickly, just as

surprised as he was that he had agreed. "I have just the local venue, a morning show and the national one can be on a weekday morning show. I'll set it up and forward you all the information. You're going to be brilliant. Trust me. It's going to be perfect."

That was yesterday morning. That evening Quinn sat in the car headed to the airport and regretted his decision. But it was too late. Nola had booked him almost immediately. After agreeing, he received her email with all the details an hour later.

Both she and Danny had been bugging him to do something. So, he finally agreed. Nola was thrilled. Danny was thrilled and his publishers were so delighted they agreed to fly him out on a private jet. The town car pulled up to the private airstrip off the airport. Quinn got out and headed to the waiting airplane. His phone rang. He grimaced seeing the caller ID. It was the main desk at the resort. They had never called him before. He answered. "Hello."

"Dr. Anderson, this is Alona at Serenity. I'm sorry to call you like this, but it is important. There's been an accident. Shay Daniels fell down High Point. She was in the emergency room all day now she's being moved here. I thought you might like to know."

Quinn stopped walking. He stood still listening intently. An ice-cold chill shot through him. His heart pounded in his chest and his hands visibly shook. "Is she okay? What happened?" he asked quickly.

"Yes, I believe she is. She's being released, so she's well enough to come back here but not to go home. I only have secondhand information about what actually happened, and it's sketchy at best. I do know that an E.R. administrator called here to confirm that she was a guest ten minutes ago. I called you as soon as I hung up with them."

He instantly turned back and headed to the car. The driver quickly scrambled to get in and looked in the rearview mirror for instructions.

"Where is she now?"

"She just got discharged. She'll be here in half an hour."

Quinn looked at the driver. "Take me to Serenity, fast." The driver nodded and sped off. "When did this happen?"

"I'm not sure. She left this morning. I personally assembled her backpack. I believe she was unconscious when she was brought in."

"I'm on my way. Call Danny and have him contact Nola and cancel tomorrow morning."

"Sure, anything else?" she asked.

"Pray."

Less than an hour later the sleek black town car pulled up out front of Serenity and Quinn got out. He rushed through the lobby to the elevators. It seemed like forever to get to the penthouse. He took a deep breath, but still he was anxious. The last sixty minutes had been hell. The driver sped like devil's fire was on his tail and still it wasn't fast enough. The elevator doors opened and Quinn walked in. Two women stood and turned as soon as he entered. "Where is she?" he asked Alona.

"Upstairs, she's asleep." Alona quickly introduced Quinn to Rose Kenner and explained it was her hiking group that found Shay. Rose had stayed at the hospital with her all day.

Quinn thanked her then glanced up at the penthouse's upper level. "How is she?"

"The doctor says she was very lucky. Thankfully nothing was broken. She does have a slight concussion, but nothing serious. She's gonna have a headache when she wakes up. Also, the doctor gave her some medicine to sleep and ease the pain. She's got bumps and bruises and some small scrapes and one cut on her leg where she hit a rock that broke her fall. She said Shay needs rest for the next few days then to come back for a final checkup. But by then she should be fine."

Quinn nodded. "Have you talked to her?"

"Yes," Alona said, smiling. "She told me she forgot to set off the flare I gave her."

Quinn smiled. It sounded exactly like something she'd say. "How did this happen?"

"She got off the path on the way down from High Point."

Quinn shook his head. He knew that area well. It wasn't the place to experiment and take shortcuts. Both Rose and Alona had to leave. Quinn thanked them again and walked them to the elevator. After they left he went upstairs to see Shay. The room was dark and she was lying in bed asleep just as Alona said. He stood a moment, relieved to see she was okay. He'd gone through hell when he found out she fell down the side of a mountain. He walked over to the bed, leaned down and stroked the side of her face lovingly. A few minutes later he came back downstairs. It was going to be a long night.

Shay stirred then woke up. She'd dreamt she fell down the side of a mountain. She tried to get up too quickly and realized she really did. She also dreamed Quinn was there. Wanting to know if that was true, too, she gingerly got out of bed and slowly went downstairs.

The smell of something incredible cooking drew her to the kitchen like a magnet. She went in and found a covered pot on the stove. She peeked inside. It was chili. She inhaled. It was the best medicine in the world. She smiled, picking up a spoon to taste. It was really meaty, crazy hot and super spicy, just like she liked it only better. She smiled and looked around. Quinn was standing in the doorway. "If I didn't know any better, I'd say you were trying to seduce me," she said, trying to sound lighthearted.

"I am, so it's a good thing you know better," he said, walking toward her. "How is it?"

"Delicious."

He shook his head slowly. She smiled knowing exactly what he was going to say. "I know, I know, not one of my more brilliant moves."

He held his hand out to her. She grasped it. He held

tight as she stepped into his embrace. "I'm just happy you're okay. How do you feel?"

"Like I fell down the side of a mountain," she said.

"Thankfully not all that way," he said, kissing her hand. "Come, get back in bed. I'll bring up dinner," he whispered. She nodded. He led her upstairs and she climbed in bed.

"There's room for two," she offered.

"When you're better," he promised.

She watched him turn to leave. "Hey," she called out. He turned to her. "I'm better," she taunted. He smiled, shaking his head. A few minutes later Quinn brought two bowls of chili, cornbread and iced tea to the bedroom. They sat on her bed and ate. She took a big spoonful and nodded until she chewed and swallowed. "This is so delicious. Did you get one of the chefs to cook it?"

"No, not this time, I made it for you," he said proudly.

"It's fantastic. What's your recipe?"

"It's an old family secret."

"How do I get it?" she asked.

"I'll think about it," he joked.

They finished the meal and he set the dishes aside. The medicine was making her sleepy, so she asked him to lie down with her. He did. She closed her eyes and snuggled closer. "When do you have to go away again?" she asked.

"The end of the week," he said.

"Five days," she muttered. A few minutes later she was fast asleep. Quinn got up, careful not to wake her.

He took the dishes down to the kitchen then grabbed his laptop and brought it into her bedroom. He worked at the desk while she slept. Her heard her stir and turned and watched her sleep.

He smiled. The moment was perfect. He was finally content. He had reached the turning point and now everything was different. She had done what he considered near impossible. She had opened his heart and for the first time in a long, long time he found what he'd been searching for: love. He'd written about it all his adult life, but it took a woman who didn't believe in romance to show him how to fall in love. Then the realization hit him. How does one tell the woman they love that it was all a scientific study? Then he considered another truth—she'd never have to know.

Chapter 15

Two days later Shay was feeling fantastic. The headaches were gone and aside from a small bandage on her leg, she was as good as new. The next two days after that passed in a rapid secession of unbelievable bliss. Each day was more exciting than the last. Quinn stayed around and together they experienced the full myriad of Serenity's vast amenities and the area's most welcoming traditions.

They played golf, visited museums, went biking and horseback riding. They attended sculpting and cooking classes and also spent an evening taking salsa lessons. They ate breakfast together and late at night they languished over elegant dinners before making love and starting the whirlwind of excitement all over again.

They talked and laughed and enjoyed everything Tucson had to offer. Each day was the start of another new exhilarating journey spent with the man she loved.

The joy of knowing that equaled the sorrow of the inevitable end. She knew in a matter of days this would all be over. She also knew she was so very in love with Quinn and she'd never be the same again. He taught her romance and seduction but most of all, she learned to love. The last day they were spending together was blanketed by the overshadowing of the unavoidable. It was a quiet morning when they set out early. Neither talked much in the car. It seemed they both had upsetting pains to rectify.

She was almost done with her series of articles. They were like nothing else she'd ever written before. She poured her heart into each sentence and knew it was the best she'd ever done. Although she didn't name her vacation lover, anyone who'd seen them together would know exactly who she was talking about. She just had two more articles to complete the series.

Their adventures culminated with Quinn driving the silver sports car to the Elgin region of Arizona. It was wine country. They passed several well-established wineries then continued to a wide open space and pulled over. They got out and looked around. It looked as if they were in the middle of nowhere. There was desert, hills, cacti and mountainous ranges in the far distance. But there were also row after row of what looked like scrawny branches held in check by metal posts and thick wire. At mid-level an irrigation drip constantly watered the now twigs and would-be grape vines.

"So this is wine country in the desert," Shay said, amazed.

"It may not seem plausible, but it's very real. Southern Arizona has some very successful wineries. They're gradually making a name for themselves and earning a reputation for excellent wines."

"But how do you grow grapes for wine in a desert? Don't you need dark, rich, fertile soil like in Sonoma or Napa?"

"Grapes are very forgiving. They grow in all types of soil. The sand mix gives the irrigation process legs which produces a nice array of sustainable grapes."

"Where are they?"

"The grapes?" he asked. She nodded. "It's March, too early for buds. But in a month or so, there will be premature canes sprouting everywhere."

"So you know grapes."

"No, I know investments."

"You bought this?" He nodded. "How big is it?"

"It's small, a little over thirty-five acres. There's a taste room and the winery over there." He pointed to the buildings across the field. Just then a man appeared and waved. Quinn waved too. "I'll be right back."

Shay nodded and watched as the two men met midway between them. They talked and looked around. She turned and walked to stand on the open plains beside the vineyard. The vast beauty of the Elgin region was breathtaking. A slight breeze blew up around her. She wrapped her jacket closer. "Are you chilly?"

She nodded. "A little."

"Are you ready to go?"

"No, not yet, it's so incredible here."

"Come, lunch is ready."

They walked down between the rows of almost grapes leading to the tasting room. Inside looked like a small brightly lit bar room with a counter, stools and empty shelves against the wall. There was also a small round table set up with dome covered plates. They ate and drank lemonade instead of wine. After lunch they headed back north to Serenity. Shay relaxed back as Quinn drove the open road. "I didn't think you were coming back before," she said out of the blue.

He knew exactly what she was talking about. That night he told her he had to be away she said goodbye with definite finality. "I know."

"Had I not fallen, would you be here now?"

"This isn't pity, Shay. Yes, I would have returned. Did I come back quicker because of the fall? Yes, I did. Am I glad I came back? Most definitely. Do I have to go back? Yes."

"More book signings," she assumed.

"No, I'm doing a lecture at the university tomorrow afternoon. It's an anthropology conference and I'm presenting a very important paper. I finally verified my conclusions."

"Ahh, another science project," she concluded quickly.

"This one is a bit more than that. It's something I've been working on for some time. It's a personal quest to answer a very difficult question."

"What's the question?"

"What is the human process of falling in love?"

"So you studied and dissected falling in love for your research," she said. He nodded. "So what's the answer?"

"That's the paper I'll be presenting."

"It sounds so clinical. Especially when you think about the human factor. Hearts are involved."

"That's very true."

"Was the conclusion what you thought it would be?"

He looked at her and smiled. "It's even better."

Shay didn't say anything for a while. She was thinking about what he said about falling in love. She could have easily given him an answer.

"There's a huge party the resort sponsors on the twentieth," Quinn said, breaking the extended silence.

"That's right, the Equinox Party. Alona told me about it. I'm looking forward to going. It sounds like fun."

"It is. You'll enjoy yourself."

"This vacation has been like a dream come true. You've made it so hard to walk away."

"Good, don't."

"Don't tempt me."

They drove the rest of the way in silence, each lost in their own thoughts. Shay relaxed into dreams of living in Arizona. When she woke up Quinn was pulling up to the front of Serenity. He parked the car and they got out and went up to the penthouse. They parted at the elevator doors just like before. And just like before, she waited a few seconds for the elevator to return. It didn't. She turned to go out on the balcony when she heard the soft beep. She turned smiling joyously. "What are you doing here? I thought you had business to take care of."

"It can wait. This can't." He crossed the room in a flash and swept her up in his arms. He kissed her like never before. "I got halfway through the lobby and turned around." He touched her face tenderly. "I love you."

Her heart nearly exploded with elation. She trembled with disbelief. Tears welled instantly and every nerve in her body shook. The words literally blew her mind. She stammered breathlessly. "I love you, too. It's crazy. It doesn't made sense. I have no idea where it came from. But it's here and I feel it."

"That's the one thing I learned. Love makes all the sense in the world. I can't remember my life before you and I can't imagine it without you. My world began again that day you turned around and smiled at me."

"Make love to me."

He looked down the length of her body, licking his lips in obvious anticipation. Their hearts had met and been sealed. He kissed her again. This time the passion was beyond measure. He devoured her unhurriedly. They made slow passionate love that would last in her heart forever. Then he left.

The next morning Shay purposely slept late. There was no real reason for her to get up early, so staying in bed until midmorning was just fine with her. She relaxed and considered the long list of resort amenities. It seemed to go on forever. She had already tried a lot of them, so nothing special really appealed to her. Reading through the booklet-style listing again, she decided to just chill.

When she finally climbed out of bed, she grabbed her robe and headed for the shower then instead chose to relax in the humongous tub. She couldn't resist a nice long soak. She set the water temperature, added bath salts and a soaking gel, adjusted and turned on the jets then got in. As soon as she dipped her shoulders below the water's surface she felt as if she'd gone to heaven. The jets hit from every direction, soothing and relaxing her body instantly. She lay back and closed her eyes in total decadence. Thoughts of seeing Quinn again stayed with her the whole time. She couldn't wait. He'd be back in twenty-four hours and their life together could begin. So why wait? The idea was a brilliant. She'd go to him now.

A few hours later Shay stood looking around excitedly. The campus was immaculate. It was exactly what Shay expected to see. The grass was neatly cut, the trees were lined perfectly and the buildings all looked as if they were glued to a game board. She parked her car in the quad and found her way to Thatcher Hall Anthropology Building. She climbed the stairs and opened the huge doors. She walked into the massive entrance hall and looked around. It was completely empty. There was white marble everywhere. Huge stone chiseled statues of lifeless men posed on pedestals all around the perimeter.

She walked up to the closest one to her and read the name. It was Charles Darwin. She continued walking, assuming they were each prominent savants in the field. On the walls were huge two-dimensional portraits, also representative of past scholars. It was exactly what she thought a psychology building would look like.

There was a security guard standing on the side watching. She walked over to him. "Hi, can you tell me where I would find Dr. Anderson? He's participating in the anthropology conference this afternoon. I believe it's in the main lecture hall."

"Sure, do you have your invitation or is your name on the attendance list?"

"No, I don't think so and I didn't realize I needed one."

"You do. Today's session is closed to the general public. You can come back tomorrow if you'd like. The rest of the conference is open to students."

"Thanks," she said, obviously disappointed, but definitely not daunted in her mission. She had every intention of walking into that conference and surprising Quinn. She just didn't know how she was going to do it. She went back outside and looked around the massive campus. Surely there had to be another way into the building.

There were several students walking past the building. Then a second group followed. She decided to follow them. She watched as both groups continued around the corner to a small door on the side. It seemed to be a side entrance. She hurried, hoping to blend in with them and not be stopped by another guard. The last person in the door, a young girl, held it for her. "Thanks, I can't believe how late I am," Shay said.

"Finals?" the young girl asked.

"No, I'm attending a conference in the main lecture hall. Do you know where that is?"

"Sure, I'm going right by there. It's right next to the library," she said, as the small group approached the side guard station. The guard was standing half watching the group approach and half watching the monitors on his desk.

"I don't have my ID."

"Don't worry about it," the young girl said. "He's usually more interested in the March Madness basketball games on the monitors than us. Chances are he'll just wave us through or possibly not even notice us." A few minutes later the guard sat back down and refocused on the small bank of monitors on his desk. He nodded the first group through then allowed Shay and the other students to pass without obstruction.

She smiled excitedly. Quinn was going to be so surprised to see her. She walked up the stairs talking easily with the young student who held the door for her.

They headed down the hall. When they came to the computer room the young girl stopped. "This is me. The lecture hall you want is around the corner right past the elevators and next to the library."

"Thanks," Shay said. "Good luck with you classes." She quickly continued down the hall and around the corner. A minute later she came to the front of the building and the main elevators. She saw a small sign directing to the library and main lecture hall. She followed the directions. Seconds later she quietly pulled the door open and stepped inside.

She was on the balcony looking down. Quinn had just been introduced. There was applause. He walked across the stage and stood at the podium. He looked gorgeous as usual. He wore a dark gray suit and stark white shirt with a silver tie. She smiled secretively. It was the tie she'd giving him their first time in Tucson.

He thanked the assembled scholars and professors then began talking about his study. She stood a moment then saw a seat nearby in the back row. She quickly sat down and listened. He started off talking about the basis of his study and its ramifications to the general population. More specifically, he talked in broad strokes about the anthropological significance of the study and the relationships of human interaction. Everything he initially talked about was basically clinical and conjectural.

After a while he began to be more specific in his findings. She listened closely. Things were beginning to sound more and more familiar. Surely he wasn't taking about her, about them. She certainly wasn't his test subject, was she?

He continued explaining his theories during each step of the hypothetical relationship. "Physical interaction," he began. He touched on the first night, then afterward, the progression and subsequent reward. She remembered the day they'd made love the first time. An icy chill shot through her body. He *was* talking about her.

The next ten minutes were like a nightmare. Everything they said, everything they did was deliberate and calculated for one specific purpose. He had everything detailed and scheduled. She was nothing more than a lab rat eating the cheese he set out for her. Her hands shook with rage and horror and her heart pounded so loud she knew the people seated next to her heard it as it finally shattered.

She sat stone-still, unable to think, speak, move, even though she wanted to. Run, scream, cry, hide, every imaginable emotion came at her all at once. Why was he doing this? How did she not know it was happening to her? Her stomach quivered and every nerve in her body tensed. No wonder he didn't want her to hear this lecture. He was talking about her. Her heart pounded in her chest as he described their first physical interaction. Her jaw dropped. He was cold and clinical, like none of it matter. She was just another experiment to be dissected and analyzed.

She looked around the room. All eyes were focused and cemented on him. Some took notes, others nodded agreeing, still others just sat absorbing every word he said. The talk continued. And every topic was their fake relationship. After a bit she lost track of time, but knew he'd been talking for quite a while.

He was preparing to sum up his final analysis when she felt the sting of tears burn in her eyes. There was no way she was going to sit here and hear the rest of her life mapped out like a textbook. She stood, turned and hurried out the same door she had entered.

She closed it silently behind her and stood pressed against it for a near lifetime. Her heart, what was left of it, was beating erratically and the breaths she took were intakes of quick gasps. Tears streamed down her cheeks. As quickly as she wiped them away, more came. She sobbed quietly. She was used to being dumped. She just wasn't used to being dumped like this.

She heard applause again and assumed he'd finished his talk. She pushed away from the door, and feeling a lot like the two-dimensional portraits and stone statues, she walked back to the elevator and headed back down to the lobby.

As soon as the doors opened she saw the guard standing at his post. He didn't look particularly surprised to see her again. "I see you found your way in. I hope it was worth it."

She shook her head. "Is it ever?" she asked, then continued passed him through the huge entrance area and then back outside. She hurried to the car she borrowed from guest services and drove away. She was focused on one thing, getting to the penthouse and then going back to New York. She followed the directions back to the resort and hurried through the lobby. She didn't want to be there when he returned. She went to guest services, but Alona wasn't there.

Remembering they also handled travel arrangements as well, she returned the car key and asked them to get her on the first available flight to New York. She went to the penthouse and started packing. The phone rang. She picked up. It was guest services with her travel information. There would be a car waiting for her in front of the resort in an hour. She could pick up her travel itinerary on her way out. She hung up. Everything she brought with her was packed. She decided to leave the other clothes. They were never hers anyway. She looked around one last time for anything she'd forgotten just as her cell rang. She pressed the answer key without looking.

Quinn smiled and shook hands with the many scholars and academic professionals in attendance. Everyone seemed excited and pleased with his findings. He was pleased, too. The easy part was done. The study was complete and his findings had been presented. Now he knew he had to face the hardest part this evening. He intended to tell Shay the whole truth. He didn't want it to get back to her any other way. Everyone wanted to talk and discuss his findings and he obliged happily. Ten minutes in, he spotted Danny looking around then heading over in his direction. "I need to speak with you," Danny said quietly.

They moved to the side. "What's up?"

His jaw clenched and tighten. "Shay was here."

"No, it's a closed session. She couldn't have gotten in."

Danny shook his head decidedly. "I don't know how, but she must have gotten in. She was here. I saw her driving away just now. I asked the guard at the entrance hall about her when I got here. He said he refused her admittance, but then a half hour later she came down in the elevator. He said she looked furious."

Quinn closed his eyes. This was exactly what he didn't want to happen. His heart trembled knowing that if she came, she would be devastated. Hopefully she stayed to the very end. "Okay," he said, and then looked around for the host. He gave his apologies then quickly left.

He hurried to his car while pulling out his cell phone. She picked up on the second ring. "You came," he said. She hung up. He called back instantly. "Shay, listen to me," he said quickly, hoping she wouldn't hang up again, "this wasn't how it was supposed to happen."

She laughed. "So how was this supposed happen, Quinn? Tell me, how could it have played out any differently? You planned and manipulated it all to this very conclusion. And you did an exceptional job. I fall in love with you. You study me the whole time. You do a lecture. Write a book about how it happened and then everyone lives happily ever after? Well, guess what, life doesn't always work like that. Everything doesn't fit under a microscope, but apparently I do. So much for happily ever after." She hung up.

Quinn drove to the resort, barely stopping the car before he jumped out. He headed to the elevator and as soon as he walked into the penthouse he heard Shay as she approached. "Just the bags there," she said, and then stopped, seeing that it was Quinn and not the bellman she requested. Quinn looked down. Her luggage was packed and waiting at the elevator. It was the visual of his world crumbling.

"You didn't stay for the conclusion."

"I didn't have to. I know the conclusion. You know what, getting dumped hurts, but getting played hurts even more. You used me." She walked away.

"Shay…" he said, following.

She turned to him fiercely, holding her hand up to quiet him. "Don't, you go back, live your life and I'll live mine."

"I can't go back. There's nothing to go back to if you're not here with me. Shay, I do love you."

"Please, the study is over, you don't have to keep pretending you love me. You have what you wanted."

"In the beginning, yes, it's what I thought I wanted. But seeing you that first moment changed everything and I didn't even know it." She didn't respond and she didn't walk away again. She just stood there looking at him in silence. "Shay…"

"You used me as a lab rat in some kind of emotional experiment," she said. Her voice was thick and broken with heartfelt emotion.

"It wasn't like that, Shay."

"Then what was it like?"

"I used myself."

"What?"

"For the study," he added. "I used myself as the guinea pig. I needed to know if I could fall in love again. I carried hurt for so long I couldn't find my heart anymore. Then I saw you that day and everything changed. You wanted me to teach you about romance, I needed you to teach me about love. I was my own subject. It couldn't work any other way. Surrounded by hundreds of people I've been alone all my life. Then you came and inspired my heart in ways I never imagined. You taught me how to feel and how to really love for the first time in my life. You're who I've been waiting for all this time. I need you. I want you. You're my life."

She opened her mouth to speak just as the elevator beep sounded. They both looked back seeing the doors open. A bellman stood looking stunned. "The bags are there. There's a car out front taking me to the airport. Thank you." He nodded and quickly gathered the bags and left.

They looked at each other one last time. Each seemed to soak in everything all at once. It was just like the first time they met. "Theia mania," he said.

"What?"

"Since the first moment I saw you. I loved you. No matter what you feel about me right now, that will never change. I feel you inside of me and I'll never let that go. You said it yourself, you never really get over the first time you really fall in love. You were right. You are that love. I'll be here when you get back."

Her heart was breaking, but she had to go. "Good-bye."

He nodded. There was nothing else he could say or do. He'd studied love a long time. It was unpredictable and unforgiving. But it was also everlasting and enduring. He knew what he felt and saw it reflected in her eyes. She loved him as much as he loved her. She needed time to feel it and know they were real.

Moments later the elevator beeped. He turned. His eyes were wide and hopeful. The doors opened and Nola and Danny stepped out. His heart instantly sank. They walked over to him.

"I heard the lecture went great," Nola said.

"Yeah, they loved it." Danny held out printed copies.

"What's this?" Quinn asked taking the papers.

"I found them online. Shay's been writing articles about her experiences here with you." Danny closed his eyes and shook his head. "They're great. It's not an interview with you or anything like that. And she never mentions you by name, but she describes being here and feeling everything she felt about falling in love. It's really good. If I was reading it, I'd want to be here and experience what she did."

"It is very good, extremely good. It's heartfelt and insightful. It reads like pure poetry," Nola said softly. "I thought we could get together and talk about some ideas I had. With her writing and your writing, bringing the two of you together is a no-brainer. I see made for TV movie all over this. Where is she?"

"She's gone."

Chapter 16

Going back to nothing was insane, but she had no choice. Shay arrived home late and decided to write the last article. She stared at the blank screen wondering what direction to go in. Then she decided to be true to her heart. Love wouldn't have it any other way. She poured her soul out confessing the love she found and experienced. She was hopeful and upbeat, ending it by leaving the door open for more. There was no sense crushing other people's hopes just because her heart had been broken. She sent the file knowing that was the end.

The next day Jade stopped by her apartment. "You are brilliant," she said, seeing Shay as soon as she opened her apartment door. She rushed on excitedly. "Oh, my

God, I can't even begin to tell you what's going on at the office. The emails are crashing the site. It crashed twice already. The network had to hire people just to keep up. Seriously, we can't keep track anymore. Your articles started something huge. It's like a soap opera and it's growing more and more every day. Someone even reenacted a scene from the wine country part on YouTube. Okay, is that insane?"

"Yeah, that's insane."

Jade was talking so fast and so excitedly she didn't notice the look on Shay's face. Finally she stopped and saw the train wreck standing before her. She reached out and hugged her friend. "Shay, call him or better yet, grab the next flight out and see him. You walked away because you were hurt. Love hurts sometimes, but it's always worth it in the end. Everything you've told me proves that he loves you just as much as you still love him. Walk, run, fly, whatever, just go back there and get your man."

"Don't start again, Jade. I don't want to think about it."

"So what, you're gonna stay in a serious funk for the next fifty years?"

"Yeah, maybe. My mom can do it, so can I. Or maybe I'll just fall in love with the next guy who knocks on my door."

"Your mom would never want this for you, not when you have a chance to be happy. He loves you and you love him," Jade said. Shay shook her head. "Fine, change of subject. You know the network has been trying to call you the last few days."

"I turned my phone off."

"You need to turn it back on. We have a meeting tomorrow."

"We?"

"Yeah, you and me, they want to see us. So, you're going to have to pull yourself together."

"I think I'll pass. I already know what they're gonna say."

Jade frowned. "What?"

"The show's cancelled what else?"

"Then why would they want to see me, too? Believe me this thing you started with the online articles is getting noticed."

Her doorbell rang. Jade, standing closest, answered. She opened the door and laughed. "Ahh, Shay, you have company."

Shay walked to the door and saw Bruce standing there with a massive bouquet of flowers in his hand. He was smiling as if nothing had happened between them. "These are for you," he offered.

"What do you want, Bruce?" Shay asked. He glanced at Jade clearly expecting her to be discreet and leave. He obviously didn't know her very well. She stood there waiting. "Well?"

"Jade, if you'll excuse us. Shay and I need to talk."

"That's okay, talk. Pretend like I'm not here," Jade said.

"No, actually we don't," Shay corrected him.

He glared at Jade. "Fine, it doesn't matter. Look, Shay, I think we need to reassess our relationship. We both moved too quickly. I think we need to get back together."

"Wouldn't your fiancée have a problem with that?"

"We're not together anymore. That's over. I was thinking we could get back together. I've read your stories online and I knew it was me you were talking about the whole time. You love me and I will grow to love you, too. You need me."

Shay looked at Jade and shook her head. Jade smiled, trying hard not to laugh. "You're right. I need to get my man."

Jade nodded. Bruce smiled. "Lock up for me." She grabbed her purse and the scarf and ran out. Then she stopped and came back to Bruce. "Um, no thanks. I have a real man who loves me and he's waiting for me."

Jade applauded.

The next flight wasn't for another few hours. Shay waited impatiently to start her life again. She arrived in Tucson hours later. It was late—well past midnight. Exhausted she grabbed a cab to the Serenity Resort. The place was alive with festivities. She'd forgotten all about the Sonora Equinox Party.

She went into the lobby where the celebration enveloped every inch of the floor. There were people everywhere. Music was playing and everyone was having a great time. Rose was there and she even saw Ham McBride, from the art gallery there. She was headed to the elevators when Alona called out to her. "Hey, you came back. I'm glad you did."

"I can't talk right now. I need to find Quinn."

"Sure, but why don't you freshen up first." Shay looked down for the first time. She was a mess, in jeans, sneakers and a T-shirt she'd been traveling in for hours. "Come on." She took her to the boutique. "I saved this for you, hoping you'd like it." It was a scarf like the one Quinn had given her the first day.

"A scarf. I have that," she said, pulling it out of her large purse.

Alona smiled. "Yes, but it's a lot more than that. It's called a camouflage. You just have to be creative. Tied correctly, you can make it just about anything you want, a dress, a skirt and top, anything."

Shay took the elevator to the penthouse. As soon as the doors opened she stepped out and looked around. The room was deep in shadows and the sheers at the balcony doors blew in the gentle breeze. She walked forward hoping Quinn was waiting. She stepped outside and saw him. Her heart raced a mile a minute. She could barely contain herself. "Quinn."

He spun around instantly. "Shay." The joy on his face was unmistakable then he stared down the long length of her body. His mouth dropped open as he looked down her body. She was wearing the scarf he'd given her and she'd been very creative.

She smiled.

He walked over and took her hands. "I've been

holding on to a hurt for too long. Meeting you helped me to let that go."

"What kind of hurt?" she asked.

"My wife was with her lover when she was killed. She'd been having an affair for months. We married right out of college because she told me she was pregnant. She said it was a miscarriage. I found out later in the autopsy, she never was." Shay touched his arm. She always assumed his marriage was a happy one. It was obvious she'd been wrong. "He romanced her, something I forgot to do. They were leaving a motel when the car was hit. They were both killed instantly."

"I'm so sorry."

"I blamed myself for so long, but not anymore."

"When I saw the photograph I thought you were still in love with her."

"No, it was never love. I didn't know what love was until the instant I saw you. I love you, Shay, with all my heart." He reached into his pocket and pulled out a ring box. "I got this just before the lecture. I was going to tell you about everything when I got back. Everything," he emphasized. "Then you came and heard. But what you didn't hear was that I told them that love had changed me in ways I'd never imagined. You changed me."

She touched his face gently. "You changed me, too."

He opened the box. "Will you marry me?"

She nodded happily. "Yes, I will." She wrapped her arms around his neck and kissed him for forever. "So, should we go to the Equinox Party downstairs? We can celebrate the beginning of spring."

"No, I have a better idea. We can stay right here and celebrate the beginning of our lives together."

She nodded. "That's the perfect idea."

* * * * *